The Arts Council
An Chomhairle Ealaíon

First published in 1999 by
Marino Books
an imprint of Mercier Press
16 Hume Street Dublin 2
Tel: (01) 661 5299; Fax: (01) 661 8583
E.mail: books@marino.ie

Trade enquiries to CMD Distribution
55A Spruce Avenue
Stillorgan Industrial Park
Blackrock County Dublin
Tel: (01) 294 2556; Fax: (01) 294 2564
E.mail: cmd@columba.ie

© Kevin Whelan 1999

ISBN 1 86023 089 X

10 9 8 7 6 5 4 3 2 1

A CIP record for this title is available
from the British Library

Cover image courtesy of the Film and
Photo Archive, Yad Vashem, Jerusalem
Cover design by Penhouse Design

Printed in Ireland by ColourBooks,
Baldoyle Industrial Estate, Dublin 13

A WONDERFUL BOY

A STORY OF THE HOLOCAUST

KEVIN WHELAN

ACKNOWLEDGEMENTS

'It is right and fitting to give thanks and praise,' goes the prayer. Each of the following has made my life better through their friendship, kindness or help:

Ken Bruen ('It is not often that someone comes along who is a true friend and a good writer.' E. B. White); Michael Gorman; Mark Kennedy; James Finlan; Dr Colm Madden; Stefanie Bringezn; the Tarpey, O'Connor and O'Sullivan families, Galway; David O'Sullivan, swimming champion, Moycullen; Des Kenny; James C. Harold; all at Charlie Byrne's Bookshop, Galway; Raymond and Paul O'Brien; Maria Dillon; Michael and Marie; the two Éamonns; my lovely god-child Fiona Whelan, Seán, Mum and Dad; all the people with impeccable taste who bought my first book, *Izzy Baia*; Jo O'Donoghue, John Spillane, Eilís O'Donoghue, Michael Brennan and Pam Coughlan, Gillian Reidy and, in particular, my editor Rachel Sirr at Marino Books; and, not least, Padre Pio ('*Ora et labora*'.)

In memory of Jonathan Ball, murdered aged three years, while visiting the shops in Warrington, England, in March 1993, and of all the other children murdered in my lifetime for adult objectives

When it is the Lord's good pleasure, the good spirits appear to others, and also to themselves, like bright lucid stars, glittering according to the quality of their charity and faith; but evil spirits appear like globules of coal-fire.

Emanuel Swedenborg, 'Memorabilia No. 7'

1

I had counted precisely eighteen kerbstones on the right-hand side of Karlstrasse the evening before, but on this February evening I had counted just seventeen. Father had walked on ahead of me. As usual he had not paid any attention to this crucial detail. 'Poppa!' I shouted. I wanted him to see this for himself. My father was, after all, Herr Dietmar Reinmayer, the respected professor of physics at the university. We were returning from there that Friday evening. On Fridays Father got off from work early. The two of us liked to walk home together, stopping on the way for chocolate cake at Muster's. Usually we took the tram but on Fridays we liked to walk. Father was waiting to cross the road. Although I was about twenty yards from him, I could plainly see that he was gripping his tattered looking briefcase with particular vigour. His knuckles had turned white. I decided that this was because he was thinking of all the stuff in the briefcase, a crazy jumble of loose-leaf pages held together in frayed paper folders, which in turn were secured with thick elastic bands. And piled in among the folders were hard, bulky books and ink-stained examination papers. 'Poppa!' I didn't budge from that missing kerbstone. Finally, he turned his head. I waited for him to smile. At last he did. Father's smile always made me feel safe.

I pointed to the place that, only the day before, had been filled by a perfectly good stone. Now all I saw in its place was a nasty rectangular gap. Clearly somebody had stolen the stone. But why would anyone do such a thing? It was this type of thinking that was not good for me. It was just this sort of thing – the missing kerbstone – that set off a mindstorm. Standing quite still, I made a quick anxiety transfer, hoping at the same time to get as far as crossing to one of my memory rooms, of which I had four. I had to think, and fast. I thrust my hands against my ears, closing my eyes for a fraction of a second, as I waited for a transfer. Nothing. The only excuse I could make for this failure was that I was standing in Karlstrasse, previously a trouble-free place for me. Besides, Father was waiting, his smile broader now. I knew then that everything was going to be all right. Still, you can never be too careful, so I clapped my hands and motioned to him. It was deeply frustrating to think that the kerbstone had disappeared like that, smile or no smile from Father. On Monday it would be the same. Then it came to me. What on earth was I worrying about? On Monday we always took the tram. The tram never passed through Karlstrasse on the way to our apartment on Berlinerallee. Such considerations were vitally important to me.

Somehow, just thinking about the kerbstones made me remember the night before. As I lowered my hands to my sides the night came back to me. It had been a night like no other. I had gone to bed early, something I did every Thursday. Father had given me my tablets with a glass of red wine, and once I was nice and warm in bed I went into a deep sleep. I slept soundly for precisely two hours, eighteen minutes and nineteen seconds. I know this because my green bedside clock told me so. But I might be wrong about the nineteen seconds. It could have been as much as twenty-two seconds. Anyway, my bedroom curtains were never fully closed. I always liked to leave a gap of exactly four inches, so that the moonlight could shine through, along with the light of the ordinary street lamps. I liked to look at the shadows on the ceiling. It fascinated me to think that the moon, way up there in outer space, sent light down to earth. To me the moon was nothing less than a giant lightbulb.

I awoke after a little over two hours, sitting bolt upright in the bed. The first thing I noticed was that the moon-shadows had left the room. My first thought was that the moon had exploded or burst like a balloon. I peered behind me to check that the curtains were still open. They were. Then I clapped my hands ten times and hummed for four seconds. Only then did I feel composed enough to climb from my warm covers and investigate. Obviously something was amiss. I gazed about the dark room, hoping to find the shadows behind me, or at least resting on the dresser. But no, there was nothing. I moved quickly to the curtains and parted them six inches. What I saw was curious to say the least. Peals of smoke rose from the streets four blocks away. Listening, I could hear the sound of revellers. Apparently a huge party was in progress. I hated parties and was only too glad that I had not been asked to attend. To the east, I saw red and yellow flames licking at the black night. All most strange. I remained standing at the window for ten minutes, picking up the clock and putting it against my ear. Its steady ticking soothed me. Putting the clock back on the dresser, I listened to the party again, satisfied at least as to an explanation for the absence of the shadows. Straining my eyes, I could just make out the shape of the moon, but all the smoke more or less blotted it from view. Now I had a sound and sensible answer to a sound and sensible question, and I was all set to return to bed and sleep when, at the end of the street, two youths appeared. They weren't much older than my fourteen years but they were passing a large bottle of wine between them. I drank wine myself, but not from the bottle like that. Between gulps they took turns roaring some horrible-sounding song. They were bad singers. I stood back from the window, watching as they were joined by six other blokes, who were also drinking and roaring. I was in my room, in the dark, and high above them. It gave me a delicious feeling, hiding there like that, knowing that they could not see me although I could clearly see all eight of them.

I noticed something about them – they all wore brown uniforms. One, the eldest by the look of him – he was certainly the most drunk – started shouting orders. He ran among them trying to get them into some sort of marching order. He said something I couldn't hear, to which one of the others replied, 'there aren't any around here.' This bloke then tipped the remainder of his bottle into his mouth, and some of the wine splashed, all black and watery, onto his collar. He made a disgusted noise before hurling the bottle to the street. When it smashed, I saw a light go on in Mrs von Sternberg's apartment and saw her peeking through the curtains. Then her light went out. I fully expected her to come racing out the door to tell them to clear off – she had a terrible temper did Mrs von Sternberg – but for some reason she stayed inside. The eight youths ran away down the street, roaring and laughing the whole way. I took one last look at the distant fires and then returned to my bed. I hoped that the shadows would be on my walls and ceiling for Friday night.

The disruption in the night meant that I woke later than usual – it was three minutes after seven, in fact. I was always most particular about getting up at seven, no later or sooner. Still, the very first thing I saw were the slanted shapes of the sun's beams over the ceiling and as always this made me happy.

Father was still waiting for me to join him to cross the road. He was pointing at his watch. With a start I realised that it must be very close to six o'clock. Dinner time. Carla – our housekeeper since mother died – would be waiting to serve our meals. In all my fourteen years I had never once missed an evening meal. Still, my mind was occupied with the problem of the missing kerbstones. Again, I thrust my hands against the sides of my head. But no, it wasn't a mindstorm. Taking my chance, I ran to Father. Ringelblum's Deli no longer displayed its pretty yellow star – I had noticed that other shops around the city had also had their yellow stars broken or taken down – and the entire front of the shop had been removed; Herr Ringelblum was tacking up a big piece of dull cloth over the empty space.

Father's right hand was outstretched, waiting to take mine, so that we were like two runners in a relay race. I opened my hand at the same instant I finished counting the windows on Ringelblum's side. There had always been nine. Now, clasping Father's hand, it occurred to me that I had counted just four.

2

When we got home, I went straight to my bedroom. There, I wasted no time going into my bedroom ritual – moving from desk to chair to wardrobe, touching each object once while humming to myself. At my desk I picked up my pen and carefully wrote my name, watching the blue ink ooze into the stained-blue blotting paper. I pulled open the wardrobe doors, peeked inside, then closed them tightly. Next, I took out my massive, five-hundred-piece jigsaw, shook the box, then put it on my desk. I hadn't decided whether I would play with it later. There was, of course, a reason for my thoroughness. I was still getting over the shock of the missing kerbstone; if it hadn't been for Father smiling and making me acutely aware of the time, I might have had a nasty mindstorm.

I sat on the edge of the bed and waited for Carla to call me to dinner. 'Andi!' I heard. I did one more quick circuit of the room, then walked carefully down the stairs. Carla was waiting for me in the hall. On seeing me, she smiled and said, 'Hello, handsome.' She always said that. Father was already at the table, a napkin tucked neatly into his collar. I took my place across from him, picking up a knife and fork and twirling them in front of my face. My reflection in the highly polished steel amused me. Carla had left the room and returned with a basket of my favourite pumpernickel bread. Then she took her place between me and Father.

'Wasn't last night something else, Herr Reinmayer?'

'A nasty business,' said Father, chewing his bread.

'You're right, Herr Reinmayer, and I for one would never condone such a thing.' She was looking at Father.

He suddenly put down his bread and looked straight at Carla. 'I hope Gert wasn't involved. Was he, Carla?' Gert was Carla's boyfriend.

'I don't know, Herr Reinmayer. No, of course not.'

'Don't let me find out otherwise, Carla.'

We finished the bread, then Carla returned to the kitchen and came back with a big pot of goulash. Father went to the sideboard for the bottle of wine he always uncorked once he was home from work. Around the table he went with it, pouring a glass for each of us while Carla spooned out the goulash. My stomach rumbled at the smell of it. Carla was a very good cook. We had been eating for – I would guess – four minutes when we heard a furious knocking at the back door. I took a sip of my wine. It was an excellent Rhine red. The banging continued. 'Do you want to answer that, Carla?' asked Father, taking an extra long mouthful from his glass. Still the banging continued. Carla just sat there. 'For God's sake, Carla, deal with him!' She leapt from the table, her face all red, and ran from the room. I could hear her talking to someone in the back kitchen.

'No, no, *no!*' she kept saying, 'They're having dinner and everything. I can't talk now!' My hearing was always very good, so I had to wonder what she meant when she said, 'I can't talk now', because it was obvious that she could talk, and was talking, 'now'. The other person must have said something, because the next thing Carla said was, 'no, you *can't* have any leftovers!' Father tore his napkin away and left the table. I got up too and followed him. Down the narrow corridor we went, until we arrived at the back kitchen. The first thing I saw was Carla trying to put someone out of the kitchen. Her face was even redder than before and she was panting like mad. Half of the body she was trying to put out wouldn't budge. I recognised Gert's bottom, bulging out of his brown trousers. Never before had I seen anyone with a bottom as fat as Gert's, or as wide. It made me think of the photograph of the moon that hung in Father's study.

I'll deal with him,' said Father, moving swiftly towards the obstruction. My father was very tall and strong – he had been a goalkeeper in his student days in Berlin – and now he took his big hands and grabbed Gert's bottom and the top of his shirt and pushed him all the way out onto the fire escape. 'Clear off, you drunken oaf!' Father shouted. Gert was no sooner gone than he was back again, this time facing the right way in. His face was all flushed and he kept looking at the floor.

'Herr Reinmayer, yes, indeed. Herr Reinmayer. Um. So very, very deeply sorry to disturb you and everything during your evening's relaxation, so very sorry . . . '

I could smell beer on his breath. I liked Gert. He worked in the chocolate factory and was always giving Carla broken chocolate bars and sweets and suchlike to take home to me. At least once a month I could expect a good-sized box of some delicious goodies. And tucked in each box was a note addressed to me from Gert. It always said the same thing: 'Eat up, Andi the Wonder Boy! Your friend in chocolate heaven, Gert.' I never understood what he meant by calling me 'Wonder Boy'. Now Gert saw me. 'Andi the Wonder Boy!' he shouted, giving me a funny salute. 'No chocolate tonight, Andi. Sorry buddy.'

'Please, Gert,' Carla was saying. There were tears in her eyes. I guess she didn't believe Gert about the chocolate.

'A late night last night, was it?' Father asked Gert.

'Quite correct, Herr Reinmayer! Go straight to the top of the class. A late night, yes, but by God a wonderful late night!' He kept leaning into and out of the doorway but only managed to stagger against the door-frame. He belched.

'Out with your patriotic friends, I don't doubt,' Father said.

'Patriotic indeed, Herr Reinmayer! Such a night for all good patriots, for all good Germans.

'Gert, *please* shut up!' said Carla. She was weeping.

'Breaking windows, setting fire to property, terrorising innocent people. You have an odd idea of what constitutes patriotic behaviour,' said Father.

'It is for the Fatherland,' said Gert, trying his best to stand straight. Father moved towards Gert and with those big hands of his he grabbed him and shoved him into the night. Then he slammed the door and turned to face Carla. 'My study, Carla. *Now*.'

'Yes, Herr Reinmayer.'

'Andi,' said Father, turning his attention to me, 'be a good boy and finish your dinner before it goes cold.' At that he led Carla from the kitchen.

3

I returned to the dinner table and sat watching steam rise from the pot of goulash. Never before had there occurred an incident like that involving Gert. It disturbed me. Now the whole evening would run late. And there was no question of me returning to my dinner before Father and Carla joined me. Besides, at 6.30 pm I was always in my room, looking at my mobiles of the solar system. Clapping my hands, I hummed and looked around the room. Then I stood up and ran around the table four times, touching Father's chair at the end of each lap. The bread had filled my stomach, and although I still had a good appetite, I decided to leave the table and make the short walk to Father's study.

'. . . of all the people, a decent girl like you, that you should have anything to do with a *buffoon* like Gert Klein.' I had my head against the study door and could hear every word.

'Herr Reinmayer,' said Carla, 'Gert's not a bad boy, not really. You see, he gets carried away when he's with his friends, like he must have been last night. Herr Reinmayer, Gert has always been one of those boys who always wants to fit in, to be popular.'

'He wants to be popular with a bunch of thugs? Carla, just think of all the decent people Gert and his friends have terrorised. Only last week a colleague of mine, Otto Brittner, was beaten up by four or five thugs in broad daylight outside his home. And not one person was charged or cautioned, whatever about being arrested. No punishment whatsoever. Think about that.'

I could hear Carla crying, making thick, choking sobs. '*Please* don't fire me, Herr Reinmayer,' she said after crying for a solid two minutes at least. 'Working here means everything to me and you know how much I love Andi.'

'Carla, I am not going to fire you. You're a decent girl, whatever about your taste in men. But there is one condition.'

'Yes?'

'That I never again see Gert Klein anywhere near my home. Your private life is your business, Carla, though I have to say that the very fact of your having anything at all to do with a person such as Gert . . . I mean, look at you, Carla. A pretty, lovely girl, who could have any man she liked, and yet you keep company with Gert. I wouldn't mind if the fellow smartened himself up a bit, even tried to lose some weight. Anything! If he did that then perhaps he wouldn't feel so compelled to hang around with a bunch of louts.'

'You're absolutely right, Herr Reinmayer,' said Carla quickly. They were silent again. I heard Father standing and I raced back to the kitchen.

'Mark my words, Carla,' Father was saying as they re-entered the dining room, 'Tell Gert Klein what I've said this evening. And try to make him lose some weight.'

'Yes, I will, certainly,' said Carla, 'and thank you, thank you. Now, let me return the food to the kitchen so that I can reheat it. Yes.' She took a tray and piled on the whole lot, including the pot of goulash. I clapped my hands at this new disruption, then took a gulp, not a sip, of wine. Father was shaking his head. A few minutes later and Carla was back. I wasted no time tucking in, mindful of the fact that my inner timetable was running a full twenty minutes late. Father refilled my glass. It was possible that the evening would have a good ending after all.

4

I switched on my bedside lamp, then sat at my desk gazing at the mobiles over the bed. Father had made them for me some years before out of cardboard. Each one was marked with its own name. At the very centre was, of course, the sun. Next, in proper order, came Mercury, Venus, Earth, and Mars. Then, far from these five, Jupiter, massive beside the others, with Saturn to its lower right, Uranus just below Saturn and Neptune beyond Uranus. But my favourite planet of all was way off to the edge of the ceiling – tiny Pluto, all by himself. I had brought my unfinished glass of wine with me. Now I moved to the armchair and settled back into it. Actually, I felt like a bit of a planet myself, planet Andreas, just to the left of solitary Pluto.

Once I actually saw one of the planets, for real I mean. It was Mars, the red planet, and I saw it from Professor Schnickel's observatory. I was ten and had never before been to such a place as an observatory. It was sort of dark inside and as silent as a church. It was seldom that I felt at peace anywhere, but in the company of Father and the professor, with the three of us taking turns to look through the telescope, I did indeed feel peace. What interested me most about the telescope was how close it brought Mars. I half expected to see it perched on the end of the telescope, and throughout the evening I would excitedly take my eye away hoping to find Mars staring back at me. I was baffled as to how a steel-and-glass tube could make magic like that, bringing something so far off into such sharp focus. However, I didn't want to think about it too much. I mean it was that kind of stuff that had a way of triggering a mindstorm. If I let it, that is. On other visits to Professor Schnickel, after gazing long and hard into deep space, I would step back and pinch myself. I'm not kidding – I'd actually pinch myself, to prove that I wasn't imagining things. I even imagined having a chat with one of the stars, and the star saying, 'Why don't you join us here in space, Andi? There's lots of room in space and everything exists here in perfect order. Best of all, there are no people, or unexpected noises, no pointless disorder.'

I returned my attention to the mobiles. They moved ever so slightly, in the wake of some obscure draught. But seeing them hanging there like that never failed to calm me. There was a knock on my door. I swung my head around, took a careful sip from my glass and went across the room to let my caller in.

'Hello, Andi. May I come in?' asked Father.

I turned from the door and went back to my place. Father entered, and as he closed the door behind him the draught caused Mars to spin, blasting Pluto against the wall. Father sat down on the edge of the bed. What I liked most about him was that I could always anticipate his movements.

'Andi, there's something you should know about.'

Mars had ceased spinning, and Pluto looked okay too. I looked back to my visitor.

'Andi, there are lots of very bad men running around the city at the moment. I've talked to you before about how our country, Germany, is at war with some other countries. And when a country is at war, Andi, well, terrible things can happen. Nasty, noisy people start popping up all over the place. That's what happened last night. The men looted and burned shops. And that's why the kerbstone was missing today, and why Ringelblum's had to replace their window. I won't go into all the whys and whatfors, Andi – it's simple yet complicated, and might only frighten you. But that's why I had to throw Gert out this evening. He is one of the noisy men.'

'Gert noisy man,' I said.

'I had no choice, Andi. You see, men like Gert, although he's always been good and kind to you, men like Gert aren't actually all that good. They're bad is what I'm trying to say. They want to hurt people, weak people usually. People like the Ringelblums, and our nice friend Herr Schnickel.'

'Telescope man space,' I said.

'The space man, yes,' said Father, smiling a bit. He didn't smile as much as he used to. 'Now, Andi,' he continued, 'these bad men are growing in number. But it's easy to spot them, because they all wear special coloured uniforms. These uniforms are either black or brown.'

'Black brown bad,' I said, understanding now.

'For now, yes.'

'Floor chocolate hat not bad.' I meant the colour of the hall floor, and of course chocolate and Father's wide-brimmed hat.

'No, Andi, all those things are perfectly good and safe. It's only the men in the uniforms who aren't safe or good that we must guard against.'

'Gert brown bad.'

'But as long as you're with dad, you'll be perfectly safe. Understand?'

'Understand safe.'

Carefully, he extended one of his hands and patted my knee. I tried not to flinch. I watched him closely. I looked at the small hollow in my trouser leg that his hand depressed. I smoothed out the cloth. Father stood. 'I'll be in the lounge if you want me for anything. There's a Beethoven symphony on the radio tonight. Why not join me and we'll listen to it together?' I looked around the room. 'I wish it was Mahler,' said Father, following my eyes around the room. 'But they won't play his music anymore.' He opened the door and looked at me for a full five seconds before closing it and walking back down the hall. Now Venus was moving swiftly. Mercury and Saturn didn't budge. Pluto knocked against the wall.

5

I slept in on Saturdays. But on the dot of 9.30 am, I left my
bed and went to the bathroom, peed, shook my willie four
times, washed my hands, being careful to rub them together
forty times, then brushed my teeth – fifteen strokes up,
twenty across. The whole ritual, from peeing to brushing,
took me exactly five minutes. In the mirror I examined my
eyes for bits of night-time sleep in the corners. I then brushed
my hair, forty heavy strokes each side. Next, I swallowed my
morning medication which had been left by the basin with
a glass of water. Two tablets, neatly arranged by the ever-
dependable Carla. Freshly laundered clothes, also courtesy
of Carla, waited on the table outside my room. Underpants,
socks, vest, a collarless shirt, tweed jacket and beige canvas
trousers. My navy-blue Saturday shoes sat at the bottom of
the pile, covered by a sheet of old newspaper. I gathered the
lot in my arms and went to my room to dress.

Downstairs, Father was enjoying his Saturday routine. I
peeked in at him in his study, where he was drinking coffee
and reading the morning paper. Bach's Suite for Lute in E
Major was on the gramophone. 'Good Morning, Andi
Reinmayer!' he called when he saw me. He was smiling. I
went into the dining room for my breakfast. I thought of
Gert and Carla and had an odd feeling about them. I was
about to butter a croissant when I noticed something odd

about the butter-dish. Holding the knife over the butter, I saw that there were three grooves already there. Father did not eat butter – he preferred margarine – and Carla never breakfasted with us on Saturdays. Who had made these three grooves? I sniffed the air. There was something not quite right about that either. A lingering odour. Gert. That was it – Gert had been at the breakfast table! I reached for the coffee pot, my hand shaking a bit, and poured myself a cup. I added milk and sugar, my attention now fixed on the bread. A whole chunk of one end of the loaf had been hacked off. Hacked, not cut. And there, just inside the door, I could see a smudge of cigarette ash. Gert. My appetite was gone. I managed to gulp back the coffee, careful not to spill a drop, although my hand was really starting to shake. I rested my head on the table and tried to work it all out. There was nothing for it but to make a transfer, and quickly, to the nearest memory room.

My memory rooms. Where would I have been without their comfort? I called them memory rooms because that's what they were – secret places inside my head where I could flee to total safety at the first hint of trouble. And trouble meant just one thing – a mindstorm. The rooms were for visiting at the disruption of a routine or ritual. There at the table I closed everything off and went straight to the first room I could think of. Apart from the sound of Bach, the apartment was silent. With no distractions, conditions were perfect. Going to one of my rooms could keep me occupied for hours, as I sat mute and still and contented. The only trouble was that it was Saturday morning. I knew that in minutes Father would be in the hall and calling me to join him for our weekly trip to the city centre. I put my hands against my head, trying to will away the grooves in the butter, the missing bread, the ash on the floor.

I would always have my memory rooms. They were as separate and whole as rooms in a regular house. I had four in all. In the first were memories of Mother, broken down into neat, easily accessible images. These accounted, in total, for two thousand, six hundred and seventy-two, assembled from the twelve years she was part of my life. Obviously there were loads more, but I thought the aforementioned figure was more than enough. There was no use overdoing it. In the second room I had fixed the view of the garden from the veranda of our old house in Wannsee. The third room was my bedroom, with a particular focus on my mobiles. Room four held the image of the old gazebo in Wannsee's park. I had once sat in that gazebo when I was eight years old and watched Mother and Father enjoying a picnic. They were laughing.

For a year after Mother died, I would busy myself scrambling through a variety of images of her, before settling on the one I liked best. Although Mother smiled and always hugged me a lot – I never minded her doing it – I decided that I would have no smiling or hugging memories of her. I did consider having memories from my regular visits to Dr Meitner's surgery though. I was just a child then but I saw a lot of Dr Meitner. I don't know why I had to see him – it wasn't like I had a tummy ache or measles or anything – but off to his surgery I'd have to go anyway. Dr Meitner never wore a white coat like a regular doctor, but sported a three-piece tweed suit instead. He always smiled whenever he saw me. He'd direct Mother to a seat near the window and have me rest on his couch. He had a long jar stuffed with liqourice sticks and he'd never forget to offer me a few, once I was nice and comfortable on the couch. I'd chew away while he peered into my eyes with this metal thing. Or he'd make me look at charts and symbols and stuff like that. It wasn't very interesting but as long as he kept the liqourice coming I never minded. When he wasn't doing his tests, he'd be busy scribbling in a notebook, muttering to himself like crazy, sometimes smiling from Mother back to me. He liked to give jigsaws, too, did Dr Meitner. When I'd finish, say, a five-hundred-piece puzzle in four minutes he would clap his hands excitedly and say, 'I could hug you, little Andreas!' Thankfully he never tried to. And not once did he take my temperature or bandage my arm or do any proper doctor stuff.

And then Mother died. Just like that. I saw her lying on her bed, all dressed in white, with her delicate hands clasped over her belly button. Wrapped around her hands were a pair of rosary beads. That day, Father dressed all in black. He kept hold of my hand through most of the day, which I didn't like all that much, but which wasn't as bad as him trying to make me bend down and kiss Mother on the forehead. 'You're never going to see her again, Andi. You might as well say goodbye now.'

It wasn't for him to know that I could see her any time I liked. I felt sad all the same, that day. The house was full of people – Grandfather Funk, Mother's father, and her brother Herbie Funk, and his wife Helga, plus what seemed like hundreds of others, mostly strangers, all dressed in black, bustling around and, worse, trying to touch me, to hold me, to bring me into their world. I didn't want to be in their world. But they just wouldn't let me alone. How I didn't have a mindstorm that day I'll never know.

In the evening, when most of the visitors had left the house, Father closed the curtains in Mother's room and left a candle burning on her bedside table. The room had become very stuffy. Some of the visitors stayed well into the night, and poor old Lotte had to keep refilling their glasses with wine or schnapps. I remember that I spent a lot of time just standing in the doorway to Mother's room, gazing at her. Her face made me think of the waxworks I'd seen during a weekend stay with my uncle, Christopher Reinmayer, who would arrive the next day from Hamburg. Mother's waxy face made me wonder if she was going to be exhibited in a museum. No one would tell me, though I knew how strange adults could be if they let themselves. And of course I never asked. I did like the way she looked, though, all nice and still and peaceful.

I returned my attention to the breakfast table. My coffee was cold but I finished it.

With Mother gone, it was Father's turn to take me to see Dr Meitner. Only, Father didn't like taking me there, at least not as much as Mother seemed to. In fact, my last visit to the doctor ended with Father leaping to his feet, from the place Mother had once occupied by the window, and pulling me from the couch, just as I was about to finish two five-hundred-piece jigsaws in just six and a half minutes. Father said something that sounded rude to the doctor and then grabbed me and together we practically ran from the surgery.

'Herr Reinmayer, Herr Reinmayer, *stop!* 'the doctor called. He came running out after us into the corridor. The floor was a highly polished linoleum. I don't know how he did it but Dr Meitner suddenly slipped and fell on his bottom onto the floor. The jolt was such that his teeth popped out of his mouth – false teeth, that is. I said before that Father wasn't much for laughing, but he laughed then as Dr Meitner scrambled around on the floor for his teeth. Then he ran to the top of the stairs, apparently with his teeth back inside his mouth. 'Andreas could be some sort of genius, Herr Reinmayer! A *genius* or some such. You've heard of such prodigies. Herr Reinmayer!' He was still saying the same thing, and at the top of his voice, when Father pushed me through the doors and out into the street. 'Please let me continue with my tests!' he cried, joining us outside. Father stopped, still with my hand in his.

'Forget it, Meitner. My son's not a performing monkey' – indeed I was not! – 'and whether you like it or not, I'm taking him home. Get someone else to experiment upon.' And that was the last I ever saw of the doctor, standing on the pavement fidgeting with his teeth and all out of breath.

'Andi?' I turned to see Father in the dining-room doorway.
'Yes,' I said.
'You've not finished your breakfast. Weren't you hungry?'
'No,' I said, looking around at the table.
'All right. But are you ready for town?'
'Yes.'
'Good boy. Get your coat. I'll meet you outside.'

6

I fetched my raincoat, being careful to put my left hand into my left sleeve first, following with the right. The door was open. Father stood on the pavement, taking deep gulps of fresh air. I stepped from the hall onto the front step, closing the door behind me. Once it was locked, I had to check that it was locked to my satisfaction. I jiggled around with the doorknob six times while humming tunelessly to myself.

Only then did I feel satisfied that I could join Father. It was a cold day. The sky was cloudless, a sure sign, I believed, that snow was due. On Kannerstrasse I saw that two shops had had their yellow stars smashed in. An army truck rumbled past. In it were men and women and children of all ages. Some of the men were old and had wispy white beards just like Father Christmas. I did not realise until then that Father Christmas lived in our city or that he had so many brothers. I wondered where they were going in the trucks – I mean I thought Father Christmas went everywhere in a sleigh with jingling bells. And where were the reindeer?

I heard babies burbling horribly under their mothers' coats. A passer-by winked at Father and me, then shouted at the people packed in the passing trucks, 'Off on your winter holidays? You bloody Jews always have all the luck!' He laughed, but I didn't hear the Jews returning his laughter. It wasn't a familiar word to me, Jew, but I guessed that the people in the trucks were Jews, whatever that meant. Something funny, I guess. Perhaps, like me, they simply didn't like change, even if it meant going on holidays or something.

'Don't stare at the people in the trucks, Andi, there's a good boy,' said Father, his voice almost a whisper.

The tram arrived and we rode it to Kapellstrasse.

Stepping off, Father and me made for Weissner's. Weissner's was where we always went for our wine and cheese and canned fruit. Lately Father always bought lots of cans of peaches and pears and stuff like that, which was strange, seeing as you could buy all that sort of stuff fresh. While he went inside to get the groceries I waited for him on the pavement. Father knew how much I detested shops. I didn't care for other people anyway, and in my experience people were always rushing around in shops, bumping into each other. In fact, over the last eighteen months, the shops always seemed to be busier, with people leaving weighed down with bags and carts and suchlike, all stuffed with food. I wondered where they managed to put it all. The women's faces made me think of Mother when she used to take me to Dr Meitner. They looked tired and sad, somehow. Close by the door to Weissner's was a beggar. He sat under the shop's awning on a little mat. His legs were only short stumps. Whenever anyone passed, he'd wriggle them, screw up his face, reach out with a grimy hand, and say, 'Lost my legs in the Great War trying to protect the Fatherland from the Yid and the Communists!' I did not know what a Yid was. I watched him. He put me in mind of a lifesize figure or something from the funfair. There was something mechanical about him. All he seemed to do was stick out his horrible hand

and run off that stuff about the 'Great War' and the 'Yid'.

He was muttering away when, out of nowhere, two men in brown uniforms appeared. They were soldiers of some sort. I did a quick transfer and thought of Father's words about the men in the black and brown uniforms. I stood back a little as the two headed for the beggar. A van pulled up and two soldiers leaped out. With them was a man in a neatly pressed black uniform. Without a word, all five of them set upon the beggar. They lifted him and threw him into the truck like a sack of potatoes or something. The beggar said, 'I'm not a bloody Yid!' and the door closed with one of the soldiers saying, 'No, you're almost worse, you worthless piece of shit!' I watched, fascinated, as the van sped away. The man in the black uniform and one of the others remained behind. Now I saw that the man in black had a big holster on his hip. In it rested a gun. He had this look on his face like he couldn't wait to fire the thing. The other bloke, the one in brown, had a rifle slung over his shoulders, the way I'd seen Grandfather Funk wear one before going hunting. Grandfather lived in the Black Forest. When we visited, he'd always take Father hunting, and I would watch them leaving the house on foggy mornings. There always seemed to be a thin covering of ice on the windows, even in spring, but off Father and Grandfather would go, returning at night laughing and smelling of beer and with a brace of rabbits or mouldy-looking pheasants strung across their backs.

Soldiers passed by Weissner's. They were dressed in grey uniforms and they too had rifles. Straight away I thought of the cowboy and Indian films I'd seen at the cinema back in Wannsee. 'Who woo!' I hollered, leaping in front of them. I don't know why I did it. That kind of behaviour was very unlike me. But I was only pretending. They stopped; grinned at me. 'Poor idiot,' said one of them, hardly bothering to look at me. His companion ruffled my hair, making my body tense and forcing me to retreat to the window of Weissner's, madly finger-combing my hair back into place, strand by strand. 'Stay indoors, kid, or the bogeyman will get you,' said the second soldier, turning away.

When Father came out of the shop he handed me a bag of shopping. But I tugged at his sleeve. 'Bogey man not get Andi?' I asked. If anyone would know, it'd be Father. Nothing was going to happen to me as long as he was around.

'Whatever made you think any bogeyman is going to get my Andi?' he asked. We started off down the street. My stomach was rumbling a bit from not having had breakfast but I didn't mind because I knew that our next stop was Kramer's Café.

'Guns hunters grandfather Funk,' I said. There seemed to be men with guns everywhere I looked.

'Those men aren't hunters, Andi. They're soldiers. Stay well away from them.'

Unusually there was a large gathering of men and women outside Kramer's. Many of them were laughing. One man kept clapping his hands and saying, 'It's true, so very true!' Another shouted, 'That's it, you tell the bastard!' Street theatre, I thought, remembering such a thing during a visit to Berlin. I hated street theatre. I hated the sounds a gathering of people made. It repulsed me, the coarse quality of their laughter. The kind that always sounded jagged and disordered, that seemed to invite chaos, with voices way off-key or just plain hideous. Thankfully, Father steered me from the group. However, instead of bypassing them, so that we could go in through the side entrance, Father marched me briskly across the street. 'Kramer's coffee cake!' I said.

'Closed, Andi,' said Father, even though I could clearly see lights on inside the café and waitresses standing in the window, all of them watching the performance outside. None of them were laughing. Father's answer wasn't good enough. I put down my bag in the middle of the road. 'Coffee,' I said, feeling a storm rising within me. I put my hands against my head.

'Look, we can have coffee in . . . Fett's!' I processed this information as I heard it. Yes, Fett's served a first-rate cup of coffee. I had enjoyed a cup there on 4 April, 1937. Then, for some reason, I felt compelled to turn my head. I wanted to see the street theatre for myself. I recognised Bernard von Manstein. Bernard had once been a student of Father's, and had even visited our house on a number of occasions, had even stayed for dinner, leaving with a book by Max Planck, who had taught Father when he was a student. 'Bernard house books!' I said to Father. I tugged at his sleeve but all he did was pick me up, right there in the middle of the street, and carry me to the other side. Then he ran back, dodging traffic, to fetch my bag. As he did I saw that he was looking directly at Bernard and Bernard was looking almost directly at him, though neither acknowledged the other. At least now I could see the entire show. One bloke had a ruler, of all things, up against Bernard's nose. And Bernard had a really massive nose. It seemed that Bernard's nose was the centre of the crowd's attention. Bernard was the street performer! And from the way he talked, you'd have thought Bernard's fellow actor was a teacher or something. 'Now students, pay attention! That's it. Regard the race's most distinguishing feature. And a fine Semitic example it is, too!' Horrible laughter followed this observation. Bernard, for his part, stood very, very still. I thought it was an odd sort of theatre, and a very strange lesson to be giving on a street corner on a Saturday morning. Looking at the man with the ruler and at Bernard, though, I couldn't help but start to laugh myself. He really did have a funny nose, did Bernard. Like when he was invited to our church to play Bach, from whatever angle you looked at him, his nose looked, well, funny.

Father returned with the bag and took my hand. Hurrying, he almost dragged me with him along the street, while in the distance I could hear the laughter and chatter of the other onlookers fading. Personally, I thought that Bernard was a hopeless actor. He really should have stuck with playing the church organ. And Father's hand was sweaty.

7

We hurried through narrow lanes near the market. Everything seemed to be spinning and each person we passed became to me a blur of discordant colour, their noise coming back to me as though through a funnel. I shook free of Father and started clapping my hands and moaning. I really had no idea where I was, other than that we were nowhere near Weissner's or Kramer's. Everything around me was confusing and alien. The mindstorm swept in, billowing through me; it thundered about my very soul. There had been no time for a transfer. And as for making it to one of my rooms, forget it. The storm ripped and rumbled. It never hurt, but I was conscious of running in closer and closer circles, my arms flailing like a crazy person, and screaming my head off. Presently a crowd gathered as I lay sprawled on the ground. The Andi Reinmayer Street Theatre. I roared, pummelling my head, stretching my mouth as wide as my jaws would let it, until the pitch in my voice broke. All the while, Father had been circling with me. I could sense his arms covering me as he held back the mob. Or should that be audience? Voices were in the air. They crashed off each other.

'Is he having some sort of fit?' 'Doubtless one of those epileptic fellows.'

'He's no epileptic.' This from Father.

'What on earth's *wrong* with the boy?' 'What sort of father are you, taking a boy out of hospital? The boy should be in a hospital, I tell you!' 'Hear, hear!' 'There are special places for unfortunates of his sort. They can be dealt with.' 'Has this happened before?' 'The poor boy. Is there anything I can do?' 'Treatment! A lad like that needs special treatment!'

A strange hand reached out for me. On contact it felt like a bolt of electricity. A female hand. I jolted back, my hands tight around my head and over my ears; anything not to hear those terrible voices. Then Father's hands were on me. I was safe. He was lifting me, although I had hardly recovered. '*Please*, son,' he whispered. I released my hands from my head and thrust my body forward, pounding my head against the pavement. Crack! Crack! Crack! Blood trickled down my forehead. Father had me over his shoulder. 'Somebody help the man!' a woman cried. He carried me to a bench, followed, of course, by the mob. On the bench, with Father's arm around me, I took the opportunity to move my tongue over the top of my lip. It came away tasting of blood. Drops hung like little balls on my eyelashes. I blinked and the mob became bathed in a watery red. 'Please, go about your business,' Father was saying. 'This isn't the first time my son has had a bad spell. Please, be on your way.' Father applied his hanky to the cut on my forehead. My brain throbbed. In a minute, the hanky was stuck in place. For the briefest of moments I saw one of my rooms assemble itself; then it faded. Father took my hand and held it to the wound. I had recovered my senses enough to see that four people, three men and a woman, were standing in an orderly line, watching me closely. The show was over but still they remained. Was it an encore they required? A man in black pushed through them. 'I heard what sounded like a fight. What's going on here?'

'He fell and hurt himself,' said Father, glancing quickly at the stranger.

'It's Herr Reinmayer, isn't it?' he asked.

'Yes, that's right,' said Father, returning his attention to me.

'Clearly you've forgotten me,' the man continued. I say 'man' although he wasn't much older than myself. Six, seven years older, perhaps. My eyes were fixed on the peculiar double cross on the armband on his sleeve. I had seen many of these strange crosses in the city. I had no idea what they meant, if anything.

'No, I've not forgotten you,' said Father. 'You're Franz Schillinger.'

'Indeed I am, Herr Reinmayer. A former student. He failed me,' he said, turning to the crowd of onlookers.

'How are you feeling, Andi?' Father asked me.

What happened to him?' asked Franz.

'He fell and hurt himself.'

'He certainly made quite a commotion. If he did just fall, I mean.'

The four spectators nodded their heads. 'That was no fall, officer,' said one of them.

'Did you take a tumble, boy?' Franz asked me.

'Boy,' I said, thinking of Mother.

'How are you feeling? That's a nasty cut you have there.' He crouched down and, very gently, put his middle finger to the hanky. He had a nice smile.

'You feeling,' I repeated.

Franz stood and said, 'This boy could have a concussion.

41

You should take him to a hospital.'

'It's really nothing serious,' said Father.

'No, it is decided. You will take him to the hospital, Herr Reinmayer.'

Father fiddled with the hanky. Apparently my cut had dried. Now I had a headache.

'Has the boy ever been treated for his disorder?'

'No. I mean, not really. There's nothing wrong with him.'

'He goes wild in the middle of a common street and you claim there's nothing *wrong* with him?' Franz turned to the others. They started nodding their heads. 'I'll tell you what I want you to do, Herr Reinmayer. The boy will be admitted to the general hospital on Monday morning. On Monday morning you will be visited by a doctor accompanied by a male nurse. And me, of course. Yes, I think a week in hospital for tests and suchlike will do the boy a power of good.'

Father's face went an odd colour at these words. He looked like he had a mouthful of vomit.

'Monday morning, Herr Reinmayer.'

'Yes. But I tell you there's nothing wrong with my son.'

'Are you *contradicting* an officer of the Reich?'

'No.'

'How do you feel, boy?' Franz asked.

'Feel now,' I said.

'Monday morning, Herr Reinmayer. Now, I'll bid you a good day. *Heil Hitler!* Suddenly he thrust out his right arm. I flinched, saw Mother in bed, and came back. Father was standing.

'Heil Hitler!' said the others.

'Herr Reinmayer, aren't you forgetting something?'

'Heil Hitler,' said Father, his voice softer than the rest.

'Herr Reinmayer, a professor of your standing shouldn't

need an ex-student, even a *failed* one' – he turned to the spectators and then back to us – 'to teach you how to salute. Now, come on, out with that arm.'

Father raised his arm. 'Heil Hitler!' he said. Everyone was nodding and smiling at Franz.

'See you Monday morning, kid,' said Franz, patting me on the shoulder and walking off.

8

After that, Father decided to cut short our visit to town. We took a tram home. Once inside the apartment, Father got on the telephone to his friend Dr Hartman. 'Bruno, please get over here, now. No, I can't explain, not here. *Yes*, it's an emergency! What? Well, in a few words, they want to take Andi.'

I was sitting in the lounge, fingering the plaster Father had applied to my forehead when the doctor arrived. They embraced each other. Father went to the drinks cabinet and poured two glasses of vodka for himself and Dr Hartman, and a glass of red wine for me. He handed the drinks around. I took a quick gulp of mine while Father and the doctor knocked theirs back in one go. This time it was the doctor who went to the cabinet; he fetched the bottle and put it on the table beside them. He poured for them both, and looked at me. 'How does your head feel, Andi?' He frowned.

'Feel,' I said.

'Does it hurt?' He reached out and gently stroked the plaster.

'Hurt.'

'Only a small bump. You'll live, Andi!' He smiled, raising his glass. 'Tell me exactly what happened, Dietmar,' he said.

'Well, as you know, Bruno, until now I've been keeping Andi occupied in my office. He helps the secretaries; they love him. Before his mother died, she had schooled him at home, and God knows she did her best. That way we succeeded in keeping him away from hospitals and the authorities. Then, this morning . . . terrible. Lately, one has become accustomed to seeing or hearing various acts of barbarism. But it's only when you see it up close, when it touches you in some way, so that it touches your life . . . I mean, it's chilling, really chilling, Bruno. What I saw this morning brought it all home to me with terrible force. I know now with absolute certainty that the Germany of my youth has gone forever. And whatever illusions I had about our people . . . They're vanished now, that's for sure. For illusions they surely were. You see, Bruno, I actually thought that Andi and I could be untouched by this madness, that so long as we kept our heads down and minded our own business . . . How very naive of me. But I'm getting off the subject. We had just left Weissner's and were on our way to Kramer's for coffee and pastries. It's something we do every Saturday without fail. Up ahead of us, outside the café, there was what I can only describe as a mob. Twenty, twenty-five, thirty people; something like that. Just your ordinary, commonplace, jeering mob. Perfectly decent-looking men and women. And somehow that's what's really frightening, Bruno; their ordinariness. That's the really scary thing. The subject of all their attention was a young fellow with an unusually big nose. Anyway, it didn't take me more than a second to see that this unfortunate was none other than a former student of mine, Bernard von Manstein. Some thug was exclaiming about Bernard's nose. Apparently he took him for a Jew. The horrible irony of it, Bruno.' I knew that what I was seeing was real, that it was happening before my

45

eyes, but it was so terrible, unfair, unreasonable . . . I had no choice but to believe what my own senses were telling me. Of course, we couldn't go near Kramer's after that. And there was no way I could have gone to Bernard's aid, God forgive me. The mob might just have decided to turn on me and, in turn, Andi. It was gut-wrenching to leave Bernard like that. So I carried Andi across the street, feeling, needless to say, a massive disgust with myself for leaving young von Manstein like that.'

He finished another glass of vodka and poured himself another.

'So, off Andi and I went, down various obscure side streets. Too late, of course; his precious ritual, his sacred routine, had been thoroughly messed up by then. So the boy had one of his bad turns. Which, naturally enough, drew a number of sightseers. It was only then that I felt, keenly, how humiliating it must be for the Jews now, and for other innocents like Bernard von Manstein. After a while, once they'd had their amusement, they drifted off, though you can be sure that some of the fools remained behind. It was then that Franz Schillinger entered the scene. He had once been a student of mine, a keen one too, but I had to fail him – I can't even recall exactly why, but I did. When I remembered him from tutorials, he seemed a timid, rather gentle youth, no better or worse than anyone else. This morning, however, I saw a new Franz Schillinger. Along he came, bustling forward, full of insane dreams about the New Order. And he was decked out in the uniform of a junior SS officer. About him was the unmistakable air of authority – and menace too. Power, Bruno. And the onlookers knew it. And worse, so did I. He recognised me immediately. Seeing

Andi, I suppose he saw his chance to avenge himself. And yet he was genuinely tender towards the boy. I'll never understand it. To cut a long story short, Bruno, Schillinger is sending a doctor and a male nurse, and an ambulance I wouldn't be surprised, here on Monday morning. He says Andi should be treated in hospital for his cut forehead. But we both know there's more to it than that. For all I know, a less than "perfect" German like Andi . . . ' Father started crying. I sipped my wine, watching him curiously.

'Don't let those bastards upset you, Dietmar. Nothing's going to happen to Andi. The most they'll do is run a few intelligence tests on him and the like. Probe that wonderful memory of his. He's just a child. He'll be safe in a hospital.'

'Better that than a . . . a camp? That's what you mean, isn't it, Bruno?'

It was late when Dr Hartman left. His last words to Father, as they stood at the front door, was something about 'pulling a few strings'. I was on my fourth glass of wine by then so I might have misheard him. I mean, what had a puppet theatre – or hospitals and camps, for all that – to do with me? Still, I liked the idea of going to see some puppets, whether it was with or without Father or the doctor.

9

I went to bed earlier than usual, at 9.15 pm. My head throbbed as it rested on the pillow. I felt the bump with my fingers. Father had given me a couple of tablets to take, to help me sleep, he said. I knocked them back with my last glass of wine. Yet, for whatever reason, I didn't sleep, at least not right then. I just lay there gazing at the ceiling, at the reassuring stretch of shadows that moved over it whenever a car passed in the street below. Then it came to me why I couldn't sleep. I had forgotten to update my list, 'Things I Hate'. Street theatre would make a perfect addition. I think I must have started the list as soon as I became fully conscious of the wider world. I kept it as complete and up-to-date as any of the files Father's secretary, Leni, kept in the cabinets in his office. By age ten I had a good-sized list compiled, filed and ready for reference.

'Things I Hate' began with one of my earliest memories of being touched by another person. Mother and Father were the main culprits, and other adults too, for no particular reason, would find excuses to pull me close to their grinning faces, faces which, then as now, did nothing so much as frighten me. And the world seemed to be filled with strange people who liked to do nothing more than pat my head and smile at me and insist on making conversation with me. Various violations of the spirit continued along these lines right through my most formative years.

I never hated people as such; rather, it was the stuff they did when they weren't thinking that bothered me. They meant well, I suppose. The second thing I added to the list was the sounds people made when eating, especially the sound of knives and forks scraping together, and the disgusting squelchy noises people made when their mouths were full of bits and pieces of food. Yuck. But there would be more, much more: car exhaust fumes, bright overhanging lights, roadworks (the sound of a drill terrified me); in fact, I hated noise of any kind, aside from that of classical music. I reserved a special revulsion for babies. I hated their bawling, their little red faces full of menace and violence. I hated too noisy boys and girls and I hated men and women who always laughed loudly. In fact, I just about detested anyone who didn't stick to a closely ordered, meticulous, thoroughly ritualised timetable. Timetables made the world less scary for me. 'Street theatre' would be a perfect addition, fitting right on the end of 'carhorns'. All in all, it became hated object number seven hundred and sixty eight.

The first time I heard a baby cry was on a shopping trip I made with Mother in Wannsee. She had to get a special dress for a party that was going to be given to celebrate Father becoming a professor. We went to a special dress shop for women. It had high ceilings and mirrors gilded in gold. I was five and Mother sat me on the end of a long counter. For two hours I watched as she tried on one dress after another. Finally, she settled on buying a big, plain pink dress. The saleswoman started packing the dress in a brown box. I found it fascinating to watch her at work. First, she took a few sheets of feathery purple paper. Then, carefully, she started folding the dress into sections. It was like watching a magic trick or something. Only she didn't rush. Then, she took the light paper and packed it around the dress. I loved that paper. It made hardly any noise at all and every one of the woman's gestures had meaning. I knew that I could trust her not to do anything crazy. The woman herself was sort of fat and square shaped and I tried to figure out how such an odd looking person could be so beautifully exact in her movements.

I focused in on her with all the intensity I could muster, and even considered putting the scene and all its images into a memory room. I might have too had the disturbance not occurred. The baby's cries took me completely by surprise. It was as though someone had detonated a bomb, right there and then inside the shop. Instantly, I felt the little monster's vicious cries striking through me. I thought that my spirit was about to be torn to bits or something. Even with the shop's high ceiling, the noise seemed to stay firmly in my area. It just went on and on! Not one of the women there, Mother included, did a thing to silence it. In fact, all they did was start cooing and ooing at the baby and smiling at each other.

My hands went up against my ears. Yet this did nothing to isolate the mounting horror of it all. The baby's wails seeped through the little gaps in my fingers and seemed to burrow deep into my brain. Moaning, I leaped from the counter as the mindstorm took control. I would have made to silence the baby only its mother blocked my path. I needed to hide, somewhere silent, safe. I spied the box that held Mother's pink dress. I soon had it and its contents in my hands, had the feathery paper flying in the air so that it floated down in pieces like brightly coloured clouds. In seconds the dress was in my hands and I ripped it, tore it with fury, using my fingers, my nails, even my teeth, the soft fabric stretching and tearing with every assault. Then six arms were on me, the baby's bawling was inside my head, and growing steadily. I felt like a country that had been invaded on all sides by a massive army.

Babies. In time I came to understand that babies were just the beginning. Babies didn't stay babies. They became grown-ups. Personally, it would have suited me just fine if they stayed the way they were – minus the noise, of course. In their little prams they were contained. Adults simply couldn't be trusted. That's all there was to it. I knew that I would always have to be vigilant around them, and to keep contact with them to a bare minimum, avoiding eye contact and all the other necessary gambits. I didn't want to encourage them, you see. No two people are exactly alike, whatever about appearances, and so they produce an inevitable chaos. People pop out of shop doorways at random, they jump onto and off moving trams, always smiling or scowling like idiots or madmen. No wonder a war started.

Confronted with people, I would retreat deep inside myself, to one of my perfect memory rooms. It took others some time to understand this. Take my uncle Herbie Funk, Mother's brother, for example. Herbie lived near Grandfather Funk in the Black Forest. Herbie Funk. He always smelled of onions – he had a market stall – and whenever he used to visit us in Wannsee he'd bring my parents lots of onions and peppers and sauerkraut and thick blocks of his special home-made goat's cheese, which always stank and which I never touched. But he'd bring me sweets, taking me on his knee (I hated that so much) so that I had no choice but to smell his stinking onion breath while he amused himself for minutes at a time staring into my eyes. But I could always outstare him. With anyone else I would have objected but Herbie had really beautiful eyes. Mother's were green but Herbie's were a kind of light blue. They were incredible, his eyes. I always felt nice and peaceful looking into them. And he had a mole up near his nose that made me think of a small furry animal or something. 'I'm your uncle Herbie, Andi. Never forget your nice uncle Herbie.'

Once, Father and I made a special trip to Berlin. It was, if I remember correctly, a Saturday, and the place was packed. We visited an old college friend of Father's and later took a tram through the city. The streets were thronged with people. It was among them that I saw Uncle Herbie. He was dressed in a white linen suit and walking hand-in-hand with a woman who was not Aunt Helga his wife. She was pretty, this strange woman, and everything Herbie said seemed to make her laugh. It was a nice laugh too. I only saw them for about six seconds – they went into a restaurant – but still I said to Father, 'Uncle Herbie pretty lady!'

'Don't be silly, Andi. Your uncle's in the Black Forest, making that revolting goat's cheese, I wouldn't doubt.'

Three weeks later, we were in the Black Forest ourselves. It was the occasion of a big family get-together. The first person I saw was Aunt Helga, running and wobbling towards us. She had a habit of hugging people and choking the life out of them but she never tried that with me. She only smiled and said that I was welcome. Herbie came out after her and when I saw him I pointed. 'Herbie pretty laughing lady Saturday!' At these words, a terrible shriek rose from

Aunt Helga. Herbie's face went as red as one of his peppers, then white, and the next thing any of us knew, poor Herbie was being chased by Helga down their long drive, and she was screaming bad words at the top of her voice, stopping only once to pick up an axe lodged in a block of wood. I never again saw Herbie. I missed his sweets, though.

10

It was Sunday, so Father and I got up early to go to Mass. I never fully understood this business of attending church. The only thing I could think of to recommend it was that everyone in the congregation behaved the same way. It was as though they were imitating each other: they spoke at the same time, stood at the same time, even knelt at the same time, all of them obeying mysterious cues given by the priest. We set off from the apartment. Something didn't feel right, however, not that there was anything unusual about that, although the events of the previous day hardly helped. As we approached the church, I couldn't seem to stop my hands going up in front of my face, as if trying to implore the shadows of order and routine to assert themselves. I thought that things might improve once we got inside the church, but they didn't. I had taken my medicine but it didn't seem to be working. I couldn't understand it. I stamped my feet.

'Not here, Andi, please,' said Father, as he took me gently by the shoulders and steered me to our usual pew in front of Our Lady's altar. I didn't know why the statue was called Our Lady. I mean she belonged to the church and not to me or anyone else. But Our Lady was what everyone called her. She wasn't a real live lady. She was a statue. I liked her for just this reason. I liked the way she looked, too, all blue and white and calm and still and silent. She was beautiful, was

Our Lady. She made me think of Mother. I made a quick anxiety transfer by focusing my attention on her for the first five minutes of the Mass, which I heard only as a dull drone. One of the altar boys dinged the bell. As the ding faded in the musty air of the church, a strange thing started to happen. My attention was focused on the statue and nothing else. And it seemed that the more I focused on her, the more real she became to me. It seemed that a subtle change overcame her features. The corners of her mouth turned up in a lovely smile. Our Lady, or so I believed, was just an ordinary plaster statue. So how on earth could she smile? But my own eyes told me that indeed she was smiling, and smiling at me, Andreas Reinmayer. She gazed deep into my eyes, like I used to do with Uncle Herbie. Everything faded until all I was conscious of was something like a shimmering light in the area of her head and face. She was trying to communicate something to me; about this I had no doubts. I smiled back. It seemed the most natural thing in the world. It was then that things got stranger still. A very peaceful, calm feeling came over me. I found myself reaching to touch the bump on my forehead; it had vanished. A tingling sensation started in my toes and spread through my body – or so it seemed. And all through this Our Lady continued to smile upon me.

I knew that I must tell Father. I tugged at his elbow. 'Poppa! Poppa, look!' I said, realising as I did that my voice had changed; the words came slower. I had spoken in the manner of the grown-ups. I tugged at Father's sleeve.

'Tell me later, Andi,' whispered Father. He returned his attention to the Mass. He didn't even look at Our Lady. When I looked again, Our Lady was as she had always been.

A simple statue. I left my place and ran up to her. If she was Our Lady, like everyone said she was, then she was mine too. Right? I grabbed at the cold plaster and shook it. Nothing happened. Frustrated, I pushed the whole thing to the ground, where it smashed into sixty-seven different pieces. Father pulled me away; I heard people gasping and watched as those around me blessed themselves. The priest, Father Reinhard, trotted over. Father started apologising. Then we hurried from the church. Outside, Father grabbed me. 'Why, Andi? Why did you have to do such a terrible thing?'

'But Poppa the lady was smiling at me!' The priest was next out of the church.

'I'm sorry, Father Reinhard. I'll pay for a new statue. I don't know what came over him. He had a bad turn in town yesterday. And now this'.

'Andi, Andi, Andi,' said the priest. 'What are we going to do with you?' Then, to Father, 'Don't fret, Dietmar. It was only a plaster statue. It is replaceable. Perhaps you should take Andi home now?'

'Yes, of course. My apologies again, Father. Goodbye.'

11

'All I want to be able to do is to understand you, Andi,' said Father as we walked home. 'I mean, son, I just wish I knew why you do some of the things you do.'

Brown-uniformed youths marched through the square, raising their legs in an oddly precise, swift movement. Arms and legs moved in perfect motion. I had witnessed the phenomenon of the marching men on a number of occasions in the past ten months. On a personal level I considered it to be a very healthy development, because it seems to be absolutely perfect in its routine, in its grave rituals. Bystanders stopped to salute them with the curious wave that Father had made in town the day before. I felt prompted to do the same, but Father had a tight grip on my right arm. I did consider, however, incorporating the soothing rhythm of their marching into one of my memory rooms.

We reached our street. Two yards from the entrance to our building stood a boy my age or possibly even younger. His face was blotchy blue. Well, it was cold after all. Nearby stood a man in a brown uniform and another man in a black uniform. I remembered what Father had said about these colours. From where I was it looked like the three were taking part in some sort of game. A game like the one Our Lady had played with me in the church. Statues. And the lucky boy had one of those pretty yellow stars pinned to his coat lapel. Father's grip had loosened. I ran off.

'Andi, come back here at once!'

'Star statue!' I told the boy. I was practically all out of breath from running. 'Statue.' I touched him on the shoulder, tugging at his star. The boy didn't budge a centimetre. The way he could stand so steadily, so free of disorder and chaos. I studied each point of the star. I wanted one of those stars; I wanted six perfect points stabbing into space. The boy stared straight ahead. Behind him was a schoolbag; its contents had been scattered all over the place. The title of one of the books was *Die Hundert Besten Gedichte*. Poetry. I wheeled around in front of him, determined to take part. Still he would not acknowledge me. I noticed now that his nose was clotted with bloody snot. 'Look at the idiot,' said the man in the black uniform.

Father caught up with me and pulled me hurriedly into the building. Glancing back I saw that the boy had started to tremble. Up the stairs we raced. On the landing Father did something most peculiar – he pulled me to him, tears in his eyes, and said, 'God give me strength but I won't let them take you from me!' Tears streaked his face. He didn't even bother trying to wipe them away or anything. I did a quick anxiety transfer, scrapped that, and drifted off to one of my rooms instead. I was back in our garden in Wannsee. We had a massive oak tree way off in the farthest corner of the garden. Long cool grass grew around that old tree and it was there that I liked to hide. In fact, I considered that tree my friend. My only friend. He was great, that tree, and why I never thought to give him a proper name I'll never know. He never moved, unless a strong wind gave him no choice, and mostly he stayed exactly where he was. Father told me that the tree had deep roots that went under the ground. Nothing could disturb that tree, whatever the weather. He always stayed in the same place. All I had to do was look out of any of the windows to the back of the house and I'd see him there. It made me feel safe, knowing the tree was always there like that. Sometimes I would rest against its cold bark. For hours and hours I could rest like that. I'd stare up through its tangled branches, even when it got dark and chilly. I didn't mind. I'd just rest there and gaze at the stars, through all those tangles of branches, so that they looked like pathways or roads in space.

'I'll never let them take you from me,' said Father when I returned my attention to the landing.

12

It was Sunday evening. The moon was out and I was looking at it through the window when Father knocked at my door. 'Andi, have you gone to bed yet?' I undressed quickly and ducked under the covers. 'Andi, I have something interesting to tell you. Please let me in.'

'In,' I called. The door creaked open and Father padded quietly across the carpet.

'You are still awake!' He was smiling. 'Good boy. Do you mind if I sit on your bed?'

I nodded and Father sat. 'Andi, I should have told you this before but there's no time like the present. Andi, you'll remember that once there was a meeting, here, in our apartment, that I conducted with some of my favourite students. We talked about Karl Schwarzschild. He was a very great man, a scientist like me. This Schwarzschild fellow had a theory. Just like you Andi he loved looking through telescopes at the wonderful things to be seen in space. He was fascinated by stars and galaxies. Anyway, he discovered that there were stars, right out there in deepest space, millions and millions of miles away, that suddenly stopped being stars. Can you imagine, Andi?'

'Imagine,' I repeated.

'Yes, Andi. These stars, well they just stopped shining. And do you know why? Even today nobody is exactly sure, but here's what our friend Schwarzchild believed. He believed that, at some point, the star just collapsed in on itself. Yes, truly! It was as though everything became too much for these stars. Think of one star, way out there in space. And one day this star thinks to itself – let's pretend here – this star looks around and thinks to itself, "I'm tired of being out here in deep space surrounded by other stars." And so he decides to do something about it. He folds in upon himself. Imagine; all that beautiful energy and light and – zap! – collapsing, like he had his own belly button and just dived in. Dived in and disappeared forever! Now, what do you think of that?'

'Star Andi.'

'My star Andi,' said Father softly. 'A beautiful star that decided to fold all its brightness away. And Schwarzchild had a special name for these collapsed, belly-button stars. Black holes he called them. And he believed that these black holes went right on shining, in their own mysterious way, long after they'd faded. They just weren't exactly the same as before, but they were still in space. Living out there, and sucking everything that came near them into their deepest core. And then spreading themselves out for miles and miles and miles. So many miles, in fact, that it's impossible to count them.' Father was crying again. 'You're my star, Andi,' he whispered. 'And when they come for you tomorrow, just remember that you'll be home soon. And that they won't be able to keep you a secret. I'll visit every day. And whenever I'm here, in your room, or visiting Herr Schnickel to look through his telescope, or studying your wonderful mobiles, I'll be thinking of you. And all I'll see is star upon star, until you return to your galaxy, home, and we can look at the stars together again.'

'Together,' I said. Father reached down to caress my head. I wanted to pull the blankets up and retreat but I didn't.

'Home soon, my star Andi,' said Father into my ear.

'Star,' I said, but I was thinking of Mother in her bed – so still and silent. Gone forever.

13

For some reason I awoke earlier than usual. I looked at the clock. It was one minute before 5 am. The street outside was silent and dark. I watched the moonshadows on my ceiling, puzzled by my wakefulness. I sat up in bed and hummed to myself. I clapped my hands. I waited. What was I waiting for? Something about the hospital. What did that mean? Was I ill? Did I need urgent medical attention? Personally, I thought that I was in good health. I felt fine. Still, the thought of going to the hospital lingered. It lingered until I consoled myself with the realisation that my time there would be like the time I spent in Dr Meitner's surgery, doing puzzles, being stared at. I was used to that. It wouldn't be so bad. At least I would be coming home at some point.

With this thought, I returned to my sleep and the next thing I knew, Father was standing in my door. He hadn't even knocked or asked to come in. He just stood there. His face was sad, even angry, yet he managed a smile. The distinct smell of cigarette smoke wafted in my door. I heard voices murmuring downstairs. I recognised Carla's and Gert's. I heard a very grown-up laugh, neither belonging to Carla nor Gert. Father sat at my desk. He wiped a tear from his face. He was silent. I went to the toilet, did my business there, took my medication and returned to the room where I dressed. 'Let's go down together,' said Father, raising his face to me and standing. He took my hand.

'Ready to hand him over?' It was Franz Schillinger, from Saturday.

'Andi the Wonder Boy!' said Gert. He was sitting at the kitchen table with his feet up, smoking like mad. He blew spirals of stinking smoke into the ceiling. He looked at Father, then took his feet down from the table.

'We have an ambulance with special people waiting to meet you, boy,' said Franz. Carla was standing behind Gert.

'He made the boy drink wine,' she said, pointing at Father.

'Is that true?' asked Franz.

'It keeps Andi calm,' said Father.

'Sounds illegal to me,' said Franz, smiling. Gert got up from his place and walked into the hall.

'Andi!' he called. 'Come here. I have a special gift for you.' Good old Gert; he never forgot me. I went into the hall and as I passed Father he put out an arm to touch me, then withdrew it. Gert was in the dimly lit hall. I saw the red end of his cigarette burning. When I was within reach of his hand – I knew that Gert would have the chocolate secreted in the other hand – he abruptly pulled me to him bringing a wad of smelly cotton wool to my nose.

14

When I next awoke I could feel, over and under me, the dry sheets of a hard bed. And everything felt and smelled like it had just been washed. For certain it wasn't my bed. Nor was the room familiar. It was big, for one thing, with high walls and a bare, shadowless ceiling. On one side was a long window of frosted glass. Now and then I could see mysterious figures passing, their feet making a clip-clop sound, the kind you make when you walk on a linoleum floor, like at Dr Meitner's. Without my beside clock, I had no idea of the time. My head felt groggy. I felt as though I had been sleeping for days. My mouth was very dry. I would have given just about anything for a glass of water. I closed my eyes and tried to make a transfer. None came. Nor any rooms. It was as if somebody had cut off the electricity to my head or something. I mean there wasn't anything there at all. 'Clip-clop' went the feet outside. I listened for a bit before falling asleep.

15

People with strange faces pushed through my room door. There appeared to be more outside my room. I could see them through the frosted glass, misshapen, like monsters out of a nightmare. Two doctors – at least they looked like doctors; they were wearing white coats – lifted me from the bed while two nurses went either side of me. I was then wheeled on a trolley into the corridor. The lights were as big as car wheels, and when I lifted my head from the trolley all I could see was more light, and the corridor, which seemed to stretch on and on. There were grown-ups everywhere and they all looked busy. A man in overalls took over from one of the doctors to push the trolley. He smiled down at me. The doctors and the nurses walked alongside us. One of the doctors gave me some tablets. 'Chew these,' he said. They had a horrible taste. All the while I kept wondering where Father was and when would he be visiting me. Would I also see Carla or Gert? Chocolate. Now I remembered. Gert in the hall. Had he given me any? Agitated, I hummed to myself and clapped my hands.

'Keep your hands down, kid,' said the man pushing me. I gripped the sides of the trolley.

'Chocolate!' I shouted.

'You can have some later,' promised one of the nurses.

We stopped at a set of swing doors. But instead of going through, the man behind me went with one of the nurses to a cubicle near the door. There was another nurse there. Various papers and things were exchanged. I was overwhelmed just then with a real sense of terror. My heart thumping – it was as though I could hear it – I raised myself from the trolley and threw myself over the bars, then hurtled through the swing doors. I ran like crazy, conscious of the storm gathering within me. Humming to myself, I ran in my nightshirt down a long, cold corridor. I was in my bare feet. I flapped my hands in front of my face and heard a nurse or someone shriek as I sprinted by. Behind me I could hear something like a riot taking place. Shouts, swearing, admonitions to stop – you name it. Heavy, adult feet pounded after me, and at one point a hairy arm came out of nowhere and took hold of my wrists, but I sunk my teeth into it, heard a scream, tasted blood, spat it out, and rushed on. Turning a corner at full speed, I saw that I was in another, apparently endless corridor. The wheel-shaped lights shone down on me and I became aware of huge rooms on both sides. The air stank of pee and sweat and disinfectant. 'Stop him, someone!' a voice cried.

Exhausted, I slumped against a doorway to one of the wards. There were children in them, some my age and others much younger. One or two of them might even have been in their twenties; I don't know. Half of them seemed to be thrashing about in their beds or jabbering like madmen. Their cries bounced off the walls and pierced my brain. I put my hands up to my ears to try to block them out. It was useless. I thrust my left hand into my mouth and bit down on my thumb. The storm was raging now and I knew that I had to let it blow itself out. But for the second time I tasted blood, all the more peculiar, and horrible, for being my own.

A mob of white coats was racing towards me. Off I went once more, looking for a release, an escape route; anything. Sunlight was streaming through a door at the end of the corridor; its light flickered off the steel cabinets and trolleys that lined the walls. With my right hand I managed to pull a trolley over. Its contents scattered all over the floor. The noise was terrible, but its effect was lessened for me because I was in the throes of a storm, although my thumb had started to throb. Still, I had put as much in the path of my pursuers as I could lay my hands on, all the while getting closer and closer to the light outside. It actually felt good to be running. Glancing back I was pleased to see that a number of my tormentors had stumbled over my traps while others were vainly trying to push the trolleys and stuff aside.

Still they came. Frantic now, I caught sight of a massive cart, set on wheels. It appeared to be full of some foul-smelling stuff. Putting my back to it, and with what felt like the last of my strength, I succeeded in toppling it over. Its contents spilled and washed down the corridor – a horrible, stinking river of brown and yellow mess. I could hear their angry cries as they slipped and fell. 'Help me, Poppa,' I said, clapping my hands in the air and making them sticky from the blood. And I wet myself. I hadn't meant to, but I was so disturbed by everything then, and my bladder was bursting anyway, that I didn't have much choice. The doors had finally opened the whole way. Light streamed through and around a figure in black. I ran to him, for some reason thinking it must be Father come to rescue me when I was hit full in the face by one of the figure's fists. And just for a moment my rooms appeared, and I saw Father and Mother smiling at me, smiling like that until everything went dark again.

16

I was strapped to a bed. My front teeth ached. I ran my tongue along one of them. It was chipped. It felt like a little blade to my tongue's probing. Raising my head, I saw that I was in a different ward. This one didn't have any frosted glass. Also, I was not alone. There were five others in there with me, also strapped down, two of whom were babbling nonsense while one struggled hopelessly against his restraints. My mouth was dry and I was starving. I closed my eyes, hoping to make a transfer. None came. My memory rooms weren't even blurs; they weren't there at all. I suppose I should have been in a terrible panic about all this but for reasons I did not understand, I wasn't. It was morning. A nurse was pushing a steel cabinet on wheels down the middle of the ward. A man in a white coat, obviously a doctor, followed her, accompanied by an older man in a grey suit.

'What's wrong with this one?' asked the man in the suit.

'Just another subnormal. Damned. Damned in the sense that he lacks that which the rest of us take for granted. Right, lad?' asked the doctor. I tried to raise myself but I was still tied down.

'Retarded,' said the nurse, approaching me with a glass of water and a tablet. The doctor loosened the straps so that I could at least sit up a bit to take a drink. The tablet was pushed into my mouth through my broken tooth. I gulped back the water, savouring every drop. It was wonderful. My gums throbbed though. I swallowed the tablet with difficulty. It tasted bitter, not unlike the kind Father gave me.

'What happened to his tooth?' asked the man in the suit.

'That, I'm afraid, was courtesy of an over-zealous SS man who was here visiting his wife. She's a doctor, not a patient.'

The three of them laughed. The doctor looked at me closely. 'This fellow isn't like the others, you know. We got hold of his doctor's notes. Not sure of a diagnosis, but there have been a number of other cases. "Village idiots" you might call them, who possess remarkable gifts in arts, mathematics, music. Baffling, really. It seems that large parts of the brain are like, well, pulp, but certain parts are highly developed, over-developed really, at a level even on a par with geniuses. And yet their manner is like that of a modern-day Kaspar Hauser.'

Indeed. Quirky, odd, bizarre. Living enigmas,' said the man in the suit.

'Or, not to put too fine a point on it: mad,' said the doctor. 'And yet,' he continued, 'they're apparently born this way. I can recall a similar case to this fellow from my student days in Stuttgart. Most curious. Fellow had the most phenomenal memory. Very distant, though. No warmth, no eye contact. Yes, the asylum was the place for him.'

'Hungry,' I interrupted.

'Don't complain,' said the doctor. 'Nurse here will look after you.'

'The asylum,' said the man in the grey suit. 'Of course, that's where most of them have been contained. Until now.' He smiled, then stopped smiling.

'Yes,' said the doctor. 'Until now.' He didn't smile at all. Then all three of them continued on their way.

17

Some time later – my stomach rumbling like mad – the nurse returned with a small breakfast of a slice of dry brown toast and a cup of coffee. She also gave me a potty to pee into. She undid the straps around my upper body so that I could sit up to eat, and when I had finished she took an apple and a bar of chocolate from her pocket and put both under my pillow. 'For later,' she said, almost in a whisper. Then she strapped me back into the bed and left the room. I immediately reached back for the chocolate and, unwrapping it hurriedly, ate the whole lot. It was nice, dark chocolate. And the coffee had been almost as good as anything Carla could have made.

I must have dozed off for a bit, because when I next awoke I was in another ward, a completely different place to before. It had windows, although half of them were frosted glass, but through the upper windows I could see the sky. It was dark. There were only four stars out. Best of all, though, I was alone, and the straps had been removed. A key turned in the door. I sat up in bed. Someone turned on the light. 'Poppa?' I called. There were two figures standing in front of the door. They switched on the light and moved closer. Doctors. One of them had blonde hair and glasses. He introduced himself as Dr Dolph Kneibel. The other had dark hair. His name was Dr Hans Huttenbach. He had a nice smile. His eyes were green. Like Mother's.

'Pee,' I said.

'What?' they both asked, laughing.

'Need pee.' Hans looked under the bed for the potty. He found it and handed it to me. I got out of bed, watching them carefully, fearful that they might shout at me, or hit my sore tooth. They didn't. Turning my back to them, I peed, staring into the frosted glass. What a relief! I put the potty back under the bed before getting back under the covers. I clapped my hands, trying to avoid eye contact with my new visitors. 'Day time?' I asked.

'What day is it?' asked Dolph. 'It's Wednesday. Wednesday evening.'

'What happened to your tooth, Andreas?' This question came from Hans.

'Man black door hit.'

'Bastards,' said Hans to Dolph. There was a desk with two chairs in the far corner of the room. The two of them carried the desk over beside the bed, then went back for the chairs.

'Andreas,' Hans began.

'Andie Reinmayer,' I said.

'Okay, Andi, we want to play some games with you. Is that all right?' asked Hans.

'All right,' I repeated.

He pulled out the desk's drawers. There were jigsaws in there. He took out one with a picture of a mountain and some woods. I got out of bed and sat on the covers, watching them. I was still in my nightshirt, a clean one, and my shoes, of all things, were at the end of the bed. It gave me a nice feeling, seeing them there like that. Hans scattered the pieces of jigsaw onto the desk. 'Do you know why you're here, Andi?' he asked.

'Here,' I said, staring at the pieces. It was a big one, five-hundred pieces.

'Any ideas?' Dolph asked. I looked at him, saw the room reflected in his glasses. Dolph had light-blue eyes. I leaned towards the desk and moved my fingers through the pieces.

'That's it, kid,' said Hans. 'You're a special boy, Andi Reinmayer. We have much to learn from you.' I began matching up bits and pieces, starting at the top, or the sky. Clumps of trees. I had a detailed image of it in my head from the cover on the box and I would reference this as I worked. I looked into Dolph's glasses and saw the room curve and flatten. They watched me work.

'Remarkable,' said Dolph.

'Fascinating,' said Hans. 'Not often we come across his kind. Let's make the most of it, see what we can learn.'

With customary meticulousness I moved left to right, right to left, until I was filling in tiny clumps of grass and a splash of blue, for a stream.

'What a waste,' said Dolph, which I thought was unfair of him seeing as I wasn't wasting one single piece of jigsaw. 'In a way, Hans, we're doing this kid a favour.'

'"We" Dolph? Keep us out of it. At least keep me out of it.'

'Don't be naive, Hans. You're as much a part of this as Herr Goebbels himself.'

'Look, he's finished already,' said Hans, nodding to me.

'And in under three minutes, too,' said Dolph, consulting his watch. Five-hundred pieces! Amazing.'

Hans had a notebook in his hand and scribbled something

in it. Dolph also had a notebook and he too scribbled in his. When Dolph finished scribbling he gave me a strange smile. Hans was smiling too, sort of. I looked directly into his eyes. He definitely had Mother's eyes. I mean his eyes were the same colour. I wouldn't want you to think that he'd stolen them from her or something. Hans didn't look like a thief.

18

Hans returned in the evening. I was sitting up in bed when I heard the key turn in the lock. I flicked my fingers and tried to visit Mother. Nothing came, only an image that was oddly blurred, like an old, faded photograph. I really think all the tablets they were giving me had a lot to do with it. I mean, they'd already made me swallow four of them that morning and afternoon. Hans closed the door behind him.

'Hello, Andi,' he said. 'Here, hide this.' He handed me a thick bar of chocolate. I put it under my pillow. I'd already eaten the apple the nurse had given me.

'Gert chocolate,' I said.

'Who's Gert? A friend of yours?'

'Friend.'

'Of your father's, perhaps?'

'Father here?'

'I'm sorry, Andi, he isn't. We're nowhere near where your father lives.' This was news to me; I didn't know what to say or think. Father said he would visit me. He said I'd be coming home soon. He had promised. Hans sat at his desk. 'Can you tell me anything about yourself, Andi?' he asked.

'Yourself,' I said, watching him open his notebook.

'Do you know why you're here?' I looked him up and down, spying a pack of playing cards in his breast-pocket. 'Do you know what's wrong with you, Andi?'

'What's wrong with you,' I said.

'I wish I knew!' He laughed. 'Do you know how old you are, Andi?'

'Old.'

'Can you tell me what your father does for a living?'

'Living.'

'Your father?'

'Father here?'

'I'm sorry, Andi, he isn't. And I don't think he will be, I'm afraid.'

'Andi afraid.'

He scribbled in his notebook.

'Cards,' I said.

'So you've spotted them! What can you play – poker, blackjack?' He took them from his pocket and started to shuffle them. I enjoyed their colours, so different to all the white and grey that surrounded me. 'I used to play quite a bit in college, Andi,' said Hans, carelessly dropping the Queen of Clubs. I watched as it drifted to the floor. Hans didn't appear to notice.

'Queen floor,' I said, looking down.

'Queen what?' He looked at his feet. 'By God but you're right! How did you see it, without me showing them to you properly, I mean.'

'I mean,' I said, quickly replaying the image of the card falling like a tiny kite. He reached down to pick it up.

'The Queen of Clubs. How did you know that?'

'Know that.'

'I'd like to try something with you, Andi,' he said. I watched him take five cards from the pack. Then, shielding them with his hand, he turned to me. Very quickly he fanned the cards before my face. I saw a blur of colours. They were: the five of Clubs, the Ace of Spades, the two of Diamonds, and the Joker. 'Can you tell me what you just saw, Andi?'

'Five clubs ace Spades two Diamonds Joker.'

'Good boy!' He patted my shoulder. I scrambled back in the bed, managed a quick transfer – I thought of the mobiles in my room – then returned my gaze to him. 'It's all right, kid! I just meant, well done. I didn't mean to frighten you.'

'Frighten you.'

'Andi, I'm going out to get Dolph – the doctor you met me with earlier – and when we come back I want you to show him how you did your trick.' He left the door open but I stayed put. In a few moments the two doctors were back.

'Don't you think that this sort of thing is just messing around?' asked Dolph.

'He's enjoying himself,' said Hans.

'Of course, we might learn something about his curious condition, although seeing how the final outcome is already decided, that does seem just a bit pointless,' said Dolph.

Hans had the playing cards out again. Behind him, in the doorway, stood a tall, muscular fellow in blue overalls. He had short bristles growing on his scalp. I could see him but the others apparently could not. He moved out of sight. I didn't like him.

'Now, Andi,' said Hans. 'I'm going show you three cards. Then I'm going to throw two of the cards in the air. Let me see if you can guess which one is missing.' Again, he fanned the cards in before me. Joker, three of Diamonds, Jack of Hearts. Then he gathered them in his fist, throwing two into the air. The Joker was missing.

'Joker,' I said before the cards hit the floor.

'Amazing,' said Dolph as Hans showed him the card tucked in his sleeve.

'Amazing indeed,' replied Hans.

'Just think of the paper we could do on him. It would make our names,' Dolph said excitedly.

'And ensure he stayed put here,' said Hans.

I noticed the man in the doorway staring intently at me. He smiled and when next I looked he was gone. A few minutes later, Hans and Dolph left. All I could hear was their excited voices echoing back to me down the corridor. No one had remembered to lock the door.

19

The man in the blue overalls came quietly into the room. He was followed by another fellow who looked like one of those American gangsters I'd seen in the cinema. It was night-time and hardly anyone passed in the corridor outside.

'All right, kid?' the blue overall man said. 'Listen, kid,' and he turned to close the door, 'I've made a bet with my buddy here, Erich. Oh, my name's Josef, by the way.' He stuck out a big, dirty hand. I didn't touch it.

Erich stood watching, rattling the change in his pockets. 'You don't wanna shakes hands with him? I can understand that, kid,' said Erich. He had an American-like accent.

Ignore him,' said Josef, sitting on the bed. 'Kid, all I want is to see you repeat that trick you did with the doctors this afternoon. The one with the missing card? Think you can do it again and win me twenty marks?' He reeked of oil and grease; his breath stank of garlic sausage and onions.

'Think you can do it, kid?' asked Erich.

'Do it,' I said.

'That's it,' said Josef, sounding excited. 'Close the door, Erich.' Erich closed the door. 'Kid, all you have to do is the same thing you did with the other two. I even brought my own cards.' From his back-pocket he took six cards. 'You watchin', Erich?'

'Get on with it. I want my money.'

'You're not going to get any. Watch.' Josef flashed the cards in front of my face. Ace of Clubs, three of Diamonds, Jack of Hearts, the Joker, the four of Clubs, the ten of Diamonds. 'Did you see them, kid?' asked Josef.

'See them.'

'Balls!' said Erich. 'There's no way he could have. The kid's an idiot. An idiot, I'm tellin' ya.'

'That's what you think. But I saw those doctors with him today, heard them talking about him. They think he's special. And I saw him do this trick and it stunned them. They couldn't stop talking about it.'

'So what? They're only gonna get rid of him, anyways. He just so much human junk. You know it, I know it, they know it. I've seen what goes on here. I *know*.'

'That mean we can't make a buck or two from him?' asked Josef. 'Are you a wonderful boy or what, kid?'

'Or what,' I said.

'Get on with it,' said Erich. 'Name the cards you just saw, kid.'

'Ace Clubs three Diamonds Jack Hearts Joker four Clubs ten Diamonds,' I said.

'See? See?', said Josef. 'Good, kid. We're halfway there. Now, I'm going to take one card away, just like the doctors did, and you have to tell Erich here which one it is I've taken – after I throw them in the air, that is.' Erich crouched down near me. He smelt sweet, like he was covered in perfume. And his pupils were dilated. They reminded me of my mobiles.

'What a sweet lookin' guy,' he said, staring at me. 'But Joe here's fulla shit, right kid?'

'Fulla shit,' I said. Erich laughed, then stood.

'He ain't as dumb as he looks, Joe,' he said.

'Ready, kid?' asked Josef. He threw the cards high in the air; I watched as they drifted down, a pretty blur of colours. The Jack of Hearts was missing. Josef scrambled around on the floor, picking up the cards like a madman. 'Tell Erich which card was missing, kid,' he said from the floor, his face all sweaty. I said nothing, but tried to make a transfer. For a fraction of a second – no more than that – I had the briefest image in one of my memory rooms of the old garden and the tree. Safety. 'Come on, kid!' said Josef, standing again to hand Erich the cards. 'See for yourself,' he told him. I was determined not to play along – whatever it was exactly that I was meant to be playing along with.

'Forget it,' said Erich, sticking the cards in his pocket. 'Let's go and get us some beers. And you can pay this time.'

'Wait a second! Give the kid a chance. Name the card, kid. You can do it I know you can.'

Erich walked to the door, jiggling away at the change in his pockets. 'I'll see you at the bar,' he called over his shoulder. 'I don't know why I let you talk me into this.'

With that, Josef swept a hand through the air, the palm smacking me full in the face. My head snapped back against the iron bars of the bedstead. I could feel heat rising in my face. 'Idiot!' he screamed, standing over me. Erich rushed across the room.

'Jesus, take it easy, Joe! He's only a retarded kid, remember? He doesn't know the answer. Just leave it.' Josef shoved Erich aside.

'A bet's a bet!' He pulled me from the bed and shook me, then dragged me across the floor and kicked me in the stomach. He let go and with his arms free started pummelling my back and chest, while I cowered in the corner, my hands over my face. I didn't want to get any more of my teeth broken. *Swish! Thwack!* went his blows. 'Name the fucking card!'

Crouched in the corner like that, I saw Erich sneaking from the room, then heard his feet pounding down the corridor. I tasted blood again; my lower lip was split. Blood speckled the walls and floor. I swallowed some blood, which was horrible, and imagined it mixing with what little food there was in my stomach. I vomited then. Gasping, crawling towards the door, I still had my attacker to contend with. Men were barging into the room, among them Erich and Hans. I don't know who the others might have been, but there were about four in all and they leaped upon Josef and there was a lot of bad words spoken and lots of gasping and tearing sounds made as they all rolled around on the floor. Finally, Josef was bundled from the room. 'All the little bastard had to do was show me the card.' That was the last thing I heard him say.

Later, a nurse came in to stitch my lip. A cleaner mopped the blood and vomit from the walls and floor. They even gave me a new nightshirt. I tried to eat some of Hans's chocolate, to relax myself, but my mouth hurt too much. I put the chocolate back under the pillow. It was only much later that I saw Hans again. He had a nasty scratch over his left eye. He knelt beside the bed, and, very gently, took one of my hands in his. 'I'm sorry, Andi,' he said. 'I'm sorry, Andi.'

20

An odd thing happened when I was asleep. All of my memory rooms came back to me, in dreams I mean, one after the other. It seemed that all I had to do was let myself drift from one room to the next. But between the rooms I thought that I could hear people crying, and with that came the sense that I was being watched by faceless figures. I must have slept through the whole of the next day – Thursday – because when I next awoke the ward was dark and the corridor quiet. My gums were no longer sore, although my lower lip was still a bit swollen. Sitting up, I flicked my fingers and hummed to myself. My mouth was very dry; I felt around for an orange that one of the nurses had left with my dinner the day before. It was small and hard but I managed to peel it with my thumbnail, relishing each juicy piece which I chewed slowly inside my dry mouth. I heard feet in the corridor. I put the orange under my pillow and sat up in bed. The key turned in the door and there stood Hans. He was dressed in a navy-blue overcoat. Underneath the coat I saw that he was wearing a thick blue pullover and black leather trousers. In his hands was a bunch of flowers and a huge, wide-brimmed hat.

'Good evening, Andi. How are you feeling?' He smiled. I touched my lower lip. 'Sore?'

'Sore,' I said.

'Here, put these on,' he said, handing me the hat and a pair of thick socks. 'We're going out.'

I got out of bed, slipped on the socks, then my shoes, then took the hat from him. Moving carefully, Hans took the hat and pulled it down so that it covered nearly half of my face. 'This has to be our little secret, Andi,' he said. Next, Hans removed his overcoat and told me to put that on also. I did as I was told. The coat felt all warm and snug from Hans's body. 'Did your Father ever take you skating, Andi?'

'Skating park circles.'

'That's the idea! Good. Because we, young man, have a date with a beautiful skater.'

I didn't know what that meant but as I looked into Hans's green eyes, I knew it didn't really matter. He made me think of Mother and yet he had Father's manner. I remembered how they had quarrelled once and Mother took me from the house and the two of us spent the afternoon and all of the evening skating in Wannsee's Volksgarten. And when it got really dark, and the only thing we could see was the skating rink lit by lamps above us, and nearly all the spectators had gone, there, suddenly, was Father, sitting by himself. And when Mother saw him he blew her a kiss and she returned the gesture with one of her own.

'Our date, Andi, is waiting. Her name is Maria. I think I'm in love with her. No, I know for certain that I'm in love with her.'

'Love,' I said.

'And I think it'll do you the world of good to get out of this dump for an hour or two. The fresh air will make you feel better.' Hans went to the door, peeked out. Then he motioned for me to join him. The coat came down nearly to my ankles. 'Andi, before we go on our adventure tonight, a few words of advice. If anyone should talk to us on the way out of here, let me do all the talking. Now I know how hard that sounds, you being such a chatterbox and everything, but still.'

We walked briskly down the long corridor, then down some stairs. To my surprise I could see the town from there. I looked for any recognisable buildings – like the spire of the cathedral – but all I saw were the vague outlines of buildings and the night sky, all black and empty of stars. Down the stairs we went, my nose thick with the smell of ammonia and old sweat. I could hear voices below us. Hans stopped. We were on another landing. The voices were coming closer. Moving me gently towards the wall and standing in front of me, Hans waited. Just then they came into view, four white-coated doctors.

'Meeting Maria tonight, Hans?' one of them called back.

'Yes. Taking the kid brother here with me. We're going skating.'

'That Maria. No one should be that beautiful. The Reich should pass a law against it!' one of the doctors called, laughing.

'Yes, indeed!' Hans called back.

When they were gone, we ran down the stairs. Down and down we went until the next thing I knew we were pushing through some EXIT doors and crossing a carpark, a thin layer of snow crunching under my feet. I took deep breaths. I felt wonderful. Hans had a motorbike. It had a sidecar.

'Ever ride in one of these, Andi?'

'No,' I said, climbing in. The sidecar felt like a little pod or a shell or something. Hans climbed on the bike. Then, carefully looking about him, he started the engine and off we went, passing through the hospital and down a long, tree-lined street. We sped past two taverns full of roaring people. They were singing and shouting. I had the hat pulled tight on my head but the wind hit my face. It felt good, and yet I was puzzled that the bike ride wasn't triggering a mindstorm. A mindstorm! I hadn't had one of those in days.

We drove into a park and Hans swung around and stopped under an overhanging beech tree. 'Here at last, Andi,' he said, stepping from the bike. 'You can take that hat off now and put this one on instead.' He handed me a woollen bobble hat. I put it on quickly, leaving the first hat in the sidecar. I looked at Hans and smiled. 'A smile from Andi Reinmayer! Whatever next?' Very gently, Hans took my hand and together we passed through a small wooden building. I could hear a waltz playing. We sat on a bench and Hans removed my shoes. Then he went to the counter for our skates. There were only six other people at the rink, and three of them were skating. One girl had long, light-brown hair tied back. She was tall and skated in a graceful arc. Then I watched as she leapt into the air and spun in the light from the lamps placed around the rink. She landed back on the ice and spun in very fast circles.

'That vision you see before you, Andi, is Maria. Isn't she just beautiful?'

'Yes,' I agreed. The waltz ended and Grieg's 'In the Hall of the Mountain King' started up.

Maria skated over to us and stopped at the fence. She kissed Hans and then turned to me. 'Is this handsome devil the famous Andi Reinmayer?'

'No devil,' I corrected her.

We put on our skates and went through the little gate that separated the spectators from the rink. Hans pushed off ahead of me, little specks of ice flying up from the blades of his skates. The other two skaters sat out the waltz, which meant we had the whole rink to ourselves. I dug my shoes into the ice and moved forward, did a semicircle around Hans and Maria, pleased by the glinting flashes their blades made as they darted about. I looked down at my skates as they threw tiny blizzards over the ice. It felt like the music was dictating my movements. I went with it. So when the music was soft, I slowed; when the tempo increased, I sped faster. I leaned into corners only to race out in a wide arc. I raced past Hans and Maria, until Maria caught up with me. Her hand went out and, hardly thinking at all, I took it. Closing my eyes, I thought of Mother, and when I opened them, there she was, in Maria's place I mean, her green eyes more beautiful than all the rituals and routines in the whole world, more beautiful than my memory rooms, than my mobiles, than the stars themselves. Looking left I saw that the five people in the spectators' stand were all smiling the way Father smiled, and they were smiling at me.

'You have a lovely smile, Andi,' Mother shouted over the noise of the wind – only it wasn't Mother's voice at all, but Maria's. I let go of her hand and spun in a circle. I must have skated for ten minutes. Then I stopped, clapped my hands, hummed for a bit, and skated over to Hans, who was taking a breather against the fence. Maria followed me over and the three of us went back through the gate to sit down. 'Where did you learn to skate so well, Andi?' she asked.

'Wannsee,' I answered.

'How would you like some hot chocolate, Andi?' asked Hans.

'Yes,' I said. Alfven's 'Swedish Rhapsody No 1' came on and for some reason filled me with sadness. I didn't feel like skating after that and removed my skates. I handed them to Maria. Hans returned with our drinks and we all sat together, not saying anything, only listening to the music.

'Help sleep,' I said, meaning the hot chocolate.

'For you, yes, Andi. But there'll be no sleep for me tonight,' said Hans.

'When are you meeting Alan and Judith?' asked Maria.

'At two. I have their papers. They'll give them safe transit out of town. Kurt and Rudi will have to take it from there. But I have a good feeling they'll get through.'

'Good, darling,' said Maria, putting her arms around him.

None of us said anything for a while. Then Hans laughed. 'I just remembered something. I bought you some flowers. I must have left them in Andi's room.'

We finished our drinks. I felt happy again. I didn't understand why.

'Give this to Judith,' said Maria, handing Hans a small parcel wrapped in orange paper.

'What is it?' asked Hans.

'Just a little gift – a bottle of Chanel No. 5.'

21

It might have been because of the excitement of my evening with Hans and Maria, but for whatever reason I slept soundly when Hans brought me back to the ward.

In the morning, I awoke to find Dolph sitting at the desk. He was cleaning his glasses. 'Don't be upset, Andi. None of this is your fault,' he said, putting his glasses back on. I thought he meant the dirt on his lenses or something.

Hans entered. 'Good morning, Andi,' he said. I was pleased to see him. 'Dolph, I've been thinking that there must be a way out for him, a loophole of some kind.'

'There are no loopholes in the Reich, Hans.'

'So you have no problem with them taking him?'

'It's for his own good.'

'But don't you ever question any of this, Dolph?'

'No, I don't. And what's more, Hans, I would keep any doubts you might have to yourself. What would your father think if he could hear you now? Our work here is crucial not just to the Fatherland but to civilisation as we know it. And as a doctor, Hans, you should be fully committed to such an ideal. Think of it: generations free of inherited maladies, diseases of both the mind and the body. A healthy race, a strong race, free of retardation and deformity.'

'And you honestly believe we can wipe out all the so-called maladies?'

'We can certainly try,' said Dolph. 'Besides, what sort of life does this kid here and his kind have? A non-life, that's what. They won't be missing anything. In fact, I happen to think we're doing them all a favour.'

'As to what we're doing with the Jews . . . ,' said Hans.

'The Jews? I agree that their fate is certainly a horrible one, but oddly fitting, I would have thought. You see, Hans, the Jew knows in his cunning heart that he's doomed. It's biblical with them.'

The two of them talked on for a bit. Finally, Dolph left, saying he had something or other to attend to. Hans stayed behind. He paced the floor, his arms folded across his chest. I guess he must have noticed me watching, because he stopped once and smiled. But it wasn't his usual, cheerful smile.

'Andi,' he said, 'if you could be anywhere right now, where would you most like to be?'

I gazed around the room, flicking my fingers and humming. Just then, the ward seemed to be just about the nicest place I could think of. I had reconciled myself to never seeing Father again. He had, after all, promised to visit me, and now he had clearly broken his promise.

'A silly question,' said Hans. 'You'd like to be home with your father, right?'

'Right,' I said. He came over and sat down on the edge of the bed. 'Nothing is going to happen to my friend Andi Reinmayer,' he said. 'Hans will see that you're safe.' He stood and, without another word, left the ward.

22

I got out of bed, had a pee, then munched on some of the chocolate Hans had given me. For some reason they had neglected to give me my breakfast, or even any medicine. I didn't mind that much because I slept through the whole morning and into the afternoon. Early in the evening I suddenly jolted myself awake. I don't know how it happened, or why, but for some reason I felt compelled to count back through the days I'd been in the hospital. I did so, calculating that it was now Friday evening. I got out of bed and, dragging the desk over to the window, I climbed on top of it to peer out. The sun was setting and below me was a convoy of army trucks. Soldiers milled about, steam coming from their open mouths. It was cold out there. I had a feeling that they were all busy, or waiting for someone or something. I climbed down, turned, spun in a few circles, like I was still at the skating rink, hummed loudly and then sat on the edge of the bed. I was waiting just like the soldiers. But for what?

Footsteps. Quick, angry footsteps. I slipped into my shoes and took a last look around the ward. I knew that it would be my last chance to do so, and I wanted to make the most of it. After my bedroom, I think it was just about the nicest, safest place I'd ever slept in.

23

In they came, three faces I'd never seen before – one a male nurse, one a doctor, and one man in a black uniform.

'You might need some help with this one,' said the doctor.

'Come on, kid,' said the nurse. 'You're coming with us.' He smiled at me. My clapping and humming had, I now realised, become the only ritual I could really depend on. So I clapped and hummed as the nurse drew me to him to brush my hair. It hadn't been combed since Sunday morning and the thick brush he produced from his coat felt great as it parted through each strand.

'He's not going to a bloody beauty pageant,' said the man in black. 'Get a move on.'

We left the ward, the three men between me, the nurse gripping my arm, but not so it hurt. There was lots of noise and commotion in the surrounding wards, odd screams and strange curses, commingled with the noise of children weeping. I felt all right, but only because the nurse was so gentle.

'Here, take this,' he said, taking a coat from a bundle stacked outside one of the wards. It was a wool-lined overcoat. 'It's cold outside.' I put on the coat and then we caught up with the other two. Outside, the air was thick with the stink of exhaust fumes from canvas-covered army trucks. Their back doors were open and people were being helped into them, including babbling children. The nurse lifted me up and another pair of arms took me and let me down on a narrow bench against the side. A clipboard was handed over and the doctor and the man in black signed it quickly. The nurse looked at me like he wanted to say something, but he didn't. He just walked away, back into the hospital.

It was fairly dark inside the van, although some light did come in from outside. The whole place was lit like the skating rink. The man in charge of us, the one with the clipboard, took a seat opposite me. I peered into the gloom. I wasn't alone. There were at least eight others in there with me, stuck down the back, and smelling fairly horrible too. And they were all older than me. At least two of them appeared to be Father's age. One bloke kept mumbling something over and over in a very dull, tedious voice. Another kept letting out a lot of very smelly farts which made some of the others laugh until the fellow in charge of us set upon him with his truncheon and, whimpering, he fell silent. One of those nearest me was a dwarf. Another had twisted legs, another did nothing but flap his arms around and rock back and forth. I would have given anything to have made a good transfer then, but nothing came.

The truck's engine started. Seconds later we were pulling out of the carpark. The other trucks curved ahead of us. I saw that we were the seventh truck in a convoy. I felt as though I was in a film, only one that was going backwards, not forwards. The truck was going in the opposite direction from the route Hans and I had taken before. We travelled along wide streets with low buildings and then passed a huge, nearly silent fountain.

For some reason I started thinking about Carla serving Father's dinner without me. Yet I felt with certainty that I would be seeing them both again on Monday morning. Also, I could even start up a few new rituals and routines, based upon my time in the hospital. Besides, I wanted to make a whole new memory room and dedicate it to my evening with Hans and Maria. The convoy was slowing down. Then it stopped abruptly. The engine rumbled away but we had definitely stopped. I looked out. We were beside a football pitch. Did they want us to play a game?

The fellow in charge leaped down from the truck and went onto the road. I could hear a motorbike. Hans drove into view. There was a sound of running feet. It was the doctor who'd accompanied me from my ward, with the nice male nurse and the man in the black uniform.

'What's the meaning of this?' asked the black-uniformed man.

'And who might you be?,' he asked Hans.

'That's Doctor Hans Huttenbach,' said the nurse, nodding at Hans.

'Apparently you haven't been told. There's been a mix-up, a mistake. That boy, there,' Hans pointed up to me, 'His name is Andreas Reinmayer. I have papers here that give me the authority to return the boy to the care of his father, Professor Dietmar Reinmayer.'

'Let me see these papers you're talking about,' said the man in black.

Hans reached inside his overcoat and pulled out an envelope. He handed it to the man, who tore it open. It looked important, this letter or whatever it was. I could see from where I was watching that it was typed. There was a red stamp or seal of some kind at the bottom. The man in black and the doctor both looked it over.

'What's so special about the Reinmayer boy?' the doctor asked.

'Do you mean you've never heard of Andi Reinmayer? Do you hear that, Andi? Well, the boy's very special, for a start. And he has the most fantastic memory. Besides, you've read the papers. Come on, let's have him. His father is waiting.' Hans had left his bike and come to the rear of the truck. He stretched out his arms. 'Come on, Andi,' he said. 'You're going home.'

I half expected the bloke in charge of us to try to stop Hans, but he made no move. In fact, he helped me down. The male nurse even rushed forward to help. Hans patted me on the back. 'Nice coat.' There were sirens coming towards us. Their wails grew louder. A car skidded to a halt and another man in black stepped out. The passenger was Dolph, but he stayed put.

'Don't make any more foolish moves, doctor,' the man in black told Hans. He marched towards us.

'Get in the sidecar, Andi. Now!' Hans said. Then he turned to the man and, almost in the same movement, he'd pulled a pistol from his coat pocket. He pointed it straight at him. The man stopped.

'Don't be hasty, Huttenbach. You're a doctor, remember? The Hippocratic oath and all that? Don't do anything you'll regret later.'

'I've had a hand in murdering the innocent. What could be more regretful than that?' asked Hans. 'Now,' he continued, addressing the others, 'I'll ask any of you armed with anything that might endanger my life to give them up, now.'

Only one person appeared to be armed and that was the bloke in charge of the truck. He threw down a handgun. The male nurse winked at me. I was nice and snug inside the sidecar by this time. 'Are you comfortable in there, Andi?' asked Hans, and he turned his head a fraction and was even smiling at me when there was a single, startling "bang-bang!" and the top left-hand corner of Hans's head just exploded. A fountain of blood and brain and bone burst into the cold air. He dropped straight to the ground, almost smiling as he went.

Dolph dropped the gun from the car's window, opened the passenger door and took off running down the road. The man in black pulled at his jacket lapels and gave an order to put me back inside the truck. I had a strange taste in my mouth, a sour, evil taste, and it was all I could do not to vomit as I was lifted back inside.

24

The nurse, looking pale, shuddered as he settled me back in my seat. It was strange, leaving Hans behind like that, bathed in the light from his motorbike, his body facedown in the ground, with just a thin layer of snow around him turning redder and redder while Hans didn't move an inch, just lay very still and dead. I kept looking out the back of the truck until he was just a tiny figure in my vision.

We pulled into a railway station – I could see train tracks – and my mood perked up, in spite of what had happened to Hans. I clapped and hummed, thinking that I was about to go on a journey like the one I had made once with Uncle Herbie and Father when we visited Uncle Christopher in Hamburg. I recalled the soothing rocking rhythm of the train as it clattered along the tracks. The man in charge lifted me down and the others followed. I looked around at my new surroundings. Over to one side were loads of men and women and children with suitcases, all wearing a yellow star. My favourite. I hoped that I would be travelling with them.

'Holidays!' I said.

'Yeah, kid, that's right: holidays,' said the bloke in charge of the truck. He wouldn't look at me, though, but I didn't mind that. There seemed to be heavily-armed soldiers everywhere. A woman at a kiosk served them hot coffee and pastries. The smell of the coffee made my stomach rumble. Orders were shouted, and I shivered, grateful for the coat. A number of soldiers had started marching the lot of us to the train. I saw cattle-cars but not regular-looking train carriages. A man with a yellow star said something about 'not being animals' and got the butt of a rifle in his teeth for his trouble, which seemed very unfair because all he'd done was make an intelligent observation. The man, his mouth bleeding, staggered a bit before heaving himself into the waiting car. A car opened for us too. From behind me came a very fat fellow, drooling at the mouth. He collapsed at the entrance to the car and started shaking. Two soldiers set about him with their rifle butts until he stopped shaking and didn't move anymore. There wasn't as much blood coming from him as there had been from Hans. In we climbed – I certainly didn't want to get another beating. There was a huge hunchbacked man right behind me.

'Take it easy, Quasimodo!' said one of the soldiers, which all the others thought was very funny indeed. He turned to look back, his huge head hanging low, peeking up and down the platform and grinning like a madman. I had retreated to the far corner of the boxcar, which even had bits and pieces of straw scattered here and there. I didn't know why they had to put me among such disagreeable people, but I didn't say anything. Being in the corner wasn't a bad place, after all. Not a bad place until the hunchback made his toilet in his pants. The stink was really horrible. Worse, he put his hands deep inside his trousers and pulled out a big pile of poo. Then, much to the delight of the watching soldiers, he started to mash it in his hands. I turned away in disgust. After about ten minutes, there were eighteen of us jammed in there. And the noise! I'd never heard anything like it. Such jabbering. And the nuttiest of the lot all seemed to gather in a clump near the doors, banging their heads off the hard wooden walls, drooling the whole time.

I felt safe enough in my corner, and even made a good transfer with the thought of the journey ahead and the calming rhythm of the speeding train. The doors were eventually slammed shut. What little light there was came in through narrow slits in the panelling. Chug, chug, chug, went the train.

Someone gave my shins a sharp kick and I stared into the semi-dark, wincing. 'Move, fool!' Above me stood a scary-looking bloke. His tongue hung out of his mouth and he had narrow, slit-like eyes. I thought he was going to kick me again but for some reason he didn't. He just shuffled off, turning his anger to the unlucky dwarf who, like me, had a nice cosy corner all to himself. The dwarf stood to let the scary man have his place.

As we left the station, I heard some of the others crying. It was terrible, the racket they made. Weeping, clapping their hands, moaning, grinding their teeth, asking for their mothers . . . The scary-looking man peed his pants. A rivulet of pee moved across the floor. I flung some straw to divert it its course, which I succeeded in doing. The hunchback walked up to me. 'Will you be my friend?' he asked.

Holding my nose, I shook my head.

'Be my friend,' he repeated.

'Friend,' I said, looking away from him. I wished there had been a window to look out of.

25

Everything about the journey got worse. And I don't just mean the noise and stink the other travellers made. A new problem was the heat. Although it was freezing outside, and I had been grateful for the coat, the temperature inside the car became something terrible after a while. I took the coat off and sat on it – the floor was still cold. I had been expecting the rocking of the train to soothe or calm me, but it did nothing of the sort. Another thing about my new surroundings I didn't like was that I had no idea of the time. No matter how hard I tried, I couldn't tell if it was seven o'clock or eight o'clock or even midnight; I hadn't a clue. But it's odd the things you can get used to, once you have no choice.

In spite of not having had any medicine that day, I didn't feel too bad. As long as the others left me alone in my own space I was okay. Some of the others were standing up against the walls peering outside but after what must have been some hours I saw two of them slide down the wall and onto the floor, where they slumped against each other. Their half-open mouths caught my attention. I realised that both men weren't breathing. The man with the narrow eyes dragged them away and took their places. I got up myself and made room beside him, hoping to get some fresh air. I peered out, happy for the cold air to rush up my nose and into my mouth.

We were in the countryside, hurtling along. There were low fields covered in snow and criss-crossed with barbed wire. I heard a noise and saw that it came from cows standing very still in the middle of a field. But I soon got bored and, stepping over a body, I returned to my corner. I was not on holiday.

26

Although my stomach had stopped rumbling, I was still starving. I had a bad headache too. Even in my corner, there really was no way to avoid the heat and the stink. The hunchback had taken to wandering around the car, shaking any sleeping body he came across and yelling 'holidays!' in their faces like it was a great joke. He was crazy. Needless to say, the dumb babbling and general carry-on of the others never stopped. I think that if, at that moment, someone had made me blind, I wouldn't have minded, because I saw something that I wouldn't have believed but that I saw it with my own eyes. The narrow-eyed bloke had fallen silent and was just lying down near the wall. The hunchback was kneeling beside him, praying – or so it appeared until I saw his face. Half grinning, half grimacing. The reason for his delight was a strip of flesh, like a badly cut piece of bacon that hung from his mouth. He was eating the dead man. I closed my eyes after that. There's only so much you can see before you have to close your eyes.

27

The train clanged to a halt. Those of us still awake, and alive, rushed to the doors. But we weren't at our destination, wherever that should turn out to be. The others returned to their places. Curious, I remained standing. We were still in the countryside, only it was much darker than before. The only light I could see came from a farmhouse beside a wood. I saw a man with a rifle – he reminded me of Grandfather Funk – walking towards the house. He stepped inside and I was close enough to them to hear a woman, his wife I suppose, and the excited chatter of children's voices. I guessed that they were in the kitchen because I could make out the flickering shadows of a fire, the shadows playing over the walls. The man had one of the children scooped up in his arms and he was kissing him on the cheek. The mother said something about dinner and then she drew the curtains and I couldn't see any more. I pictured them all sitting around the dinner table, just like Father and Carla and me did. Used to, I suppose that should be. Like we used to.

The train started to pull away again and I watched as we left the house and its occupants behind, until it was just a speck of light in the dark and then it wasn't there and all I could see was the night, as dark as ever.

28

Father had once shown me a picture of an iceberg. 'You'll like this, Andi,' I remember him saying. 'See how the iceberg is floating all by itself in the sea?' I must have given over hours to studying that picture. It wasn't a particularly remarkable picture or anything – it wasn't a picture of a star – but it fascinated me all the same. And the more I studied it the greater became my identification with its freezing mass. Throughout the journey, my mind kept going back to that picture, to its glacial beauty. Why I'd never thought to make a memory room of it I'll never know.

I turned my thoughts inward, to myself. I began to think of myself as being like that iceberg, but also as being like a secret letter, all sealed up, or the collapsed stars Father had told me about, or someone who lived inside a cocoon of his own making. Safe. Only I wasn't safe, not really. I closed my eyes and imagined myself in a boat bobbing towards the iceberg. The iceberg was sanctuary. If I could get there in my mind, I might be all right. I saw myself getting closer and closer to it. The water around me was freezing cold but that didn't worry me. I was getting nearer and nearer. I could see its brilliant, shiny sides, like mirrors. And then I saw myself. My face stared back at me. And Father's and Mother's did too. We were all together again. The only bad thing was that Father was the only one with his eyes open. Mother's and mine were closed, and our mouths hung open; it was hard to interpret our expressions; hunger or relief perhaps; or horror, mute, helpless horror.

29

One of my fellow passengers rushed forward, waking me from my reverie. He held a stinking hand in front of my face. Between his fingers something wriggled. It was a creepy-crawly of some sort, a beetle perhaps. 'Want one, pretty boy?' he asked, popping the foul thing into his mouth and chewing. All I wanted to do was retreat and to keep on retreating, to become part of the car, anything at all. I felt very weak and knew that I could not refuse the offer of food, however repulsive. He picked a fresh one from the floor. I took it from him and chewed, swallowing hard. My mouth was very dry so it wasn't easy to get down. He gave a high-pitched laugh then wandered back to his own place. Still hungry, I got up to find him. I wanted some more. Yet when I moved in his direction, the others, those who were still alive, kicked out at me. They would probably have spat too, only their mouths were dry too.

The train was stopping for the second time. Suddenly, without warning , the doors swung open. Weak and all as I was, I made a rush for the fresh air, and tumbled out onto the platform. We had arrived at a camp of some kind. There were tall towers and in the towers were soldiers with machine guns. Pylons blazed with light. And there was a high fence with barbed wire curled along the top.

'There's one who can't wait,' said a soldier, pointing to

me. In my rush to get out of the car, I had forgotten my coat. I managed to stand and, even though it was freezing, I took deep gulps of fresh air. It felt wonderful. I saw that, beyond the fence, were several low, tidy-looking huts. There was a lot going on further up the platform. Car doors being slid open, people staggering all over the place, some being helped down, others stepping off, slowly. One of the men in my car had a hard time getting from the car to the platform. I hadn't noticed him before, but there was something wrong with his legs. A soldier roared at him to hurry up, but he couldn't. A man in a black uniform strode up. 'What's taking him so long?'

The soldier shrugged. 'A cripple,' he said. The man in the black uniform took a pistol from his holster and, putting the gun's muzzle against the cripple's head, he pressed the trigger. I counted seventeen different-sized bone fragments exploding from his head; his body flopped back as blood pooled around him to mix with the mess on the floor from the other bodies inside the car. My bowels felt very weak then and I was genuinely worried that I would soil myself. Thankfully I didn't.

'Did you see that?' one of the soldiers said as the black-uniformed man re-holstered his pistol. 'His fucking head must have been made from balsa wood! Even an idiot's skull is made of sub-standard stuff.'

A doctor appeared. 'Get them into line. How many of them are there?' he asked.

'Twelve, doctor,' said the soldier. 'Though it looks like a few of them didn't survive the trip.'

'All of you will have a change of clothes once you've been deloused and had your showers. Move them out.'

This was excellent news. I was starting to itch like mad. The soldiers organised us into a line. Then we were marched through the gate. They led us to one of the huts. Without having to be told, we undressed. I took off my shoes and put them neatly beside my nightshirt. The doctor came in and forced my mouth open. He examined my teeth. I wondered if this meant he was going to do something about the one I'd broken in the hospital. At any other time I might have protested, but I was too tired. Shivering, my hands over my privates, I was moved off again. I didn't really mind being naked because I was glad to be out of that flea-bitten nightshirt.

Now I could see the shower room, some twelve yards from me. I think that we all must have seen it at the same time because we all quickened our pace, even the hunchback. A heavy steel door had been opened and at either side of it stood two skinny hospital-orderly types. In we all went, followed by many others from the train – old men and women, even a few mothers clutching babies to their chests. The floor was freezing under my feet. I looked around me at the filthy, peeling walls. It was a very dirty shower room. I hoped that they would provide us with scrubbing brushes and flannels. The ceiling was dirty too, and bare of ordinary-looking nozzles. Instead there were a number of circular holes.

I had counted twelve when the steel door slammed closed behind me.